THE GREAT SECRET

SELECTED FICTION WORKS BY
L. RON HUBBARD

FANTASY
The Case of the Friendly Corpse
Death's Deputy
Fear
The Ghoul
The Indigestible Triton
Slaves of Sleep & The Masters of Sleep
Typewriter in the Sky
The Ultimate Adventure

SCIENCE FICTION
Battlefield Earth
The Conquest of Space
The End Is Not Yet
Final Blackout
The Kilkenny Cats
The Kingslayer
The Mission Earth Dekalogy*
Ole Doc Methuselah
To the Stars

ADVENTURE
The Hell Job series

WESTERN
Buckskin Brigades
Empty Saddles
Guns of Mark Jardine
Hot Lead Payoff

A full list of L. Ron Hubbard's
novellas and short stories is provided at the back.

*Dekalogy—a group of ten volumes

L. RON HUBBARD

The GREAT SECRET

GALAXY
PRESS

Published by
Galaxy Press, LLC
7051 Hollywood Boulevard, Suite 200
Hollywood, CA 90028

Printed in the United States of America.

ISBN-10 1-59212-371-6
ISBN-13 978-1-59212-371-1

Library of Congress Control Number: 2007927526

CONTENTS

Stories from Pulp Fiction's Golden Age

AND it *was* a golden age. The 1930s and 1940s were a vibrant, seminal time for a gigantic audience of eager readers, probably the largest per capita audience of readers in American history. The magazine racks were chock-full of publications with ragged trims, garish cover art, cheap brown pulp paper, low cover prices—and the most excitement you could hold in your hands.

"Pulp" magazines, named for their rough-cut, pulpwood paper, were a vehicle for more amazing tales than Scheherazade could have told in a million and one nights. Set apart from higher-class "slick" magazines, printed on fancy glossy paper with quality artwork and superior production values, the pulps were for the "rest of us," adventure story after adventure story for people who liked to *read.* Pulp fiction authors were no-holds-barred entertainers—real storytellers. They were more interested in a thrilling plot twist, a horrific villain or a white-knuckle adventure than they were in lavish prose or convoluted metaphors.

The sheer volume of tales released during this wondrous golden age remains unmatched in any other period of literary history—hundreds of thousands of published stories in over nine hundred different magazines. Some titles lasted only an issue or two; many magazines succumbed to paper shortages during World War II, while others endured for decades yet. Pulp fiction remains as a treasure trove of stories you can read, stories you can love, stories you can remember. The stories were driven by plot and character, with grand heroes, terrible villains, beautiful damsels (often in distress), diabolical plots, amazing places, breathless romances. The readers wanted to be taken beyond the mundane, to live adventures far removed from their ordinary lives—and the pulps rarely failed to deliver.

In that regard, pulp fiction stands in the tradition of all memorable literature. For as history has shown, good stories are much more than fancy prose. William Shakespeare, Charles Dickens, Jules Verne, Alexandre Dumas—many of the greatest literary figures wrote their fiction for the readers, not simply literary colleagues and academic admirers. And writers for pulp magazines were no exception. These publications reached an audience that dwarfed the circulations of today's short story magazines. Issues of the pulps were scooped up and read by over thirty million avid readers each month.

Because pulp fiction writers were often paid no more than a cent a word, they had to become prolific or starve. They also had to write aggressively. As Richard Kyle, publisher and editor of *Argosy*, the first and most long-lived of the pulps, so pointedly explained: "The pulp magazine writers, the best of them, worked for markets that did not write for critics or attempt to satisfy timid advertisers. Not having to answer to anyone other than their readers, they wrote about human beings on the edges of the unknown, in those new lands the future would explore. They wrote for what we would become, not for what we had already been."

Some of the more lasting names that graced the pulps include H. P. Lovecraft, Edgar Rice Burroughs, Robert E. Howard, Max Brand, Louis L'Amour, Elmore Leonard, Dashiell Hammett, Raymond Chandler, Erle Stanley Gardner, John D. MacDonald, Ray Bradbury, Isaac Asimov, Robert Heinlein—and, of course, L. Ron Hubbard.

In a word, he was among the most prolific and popular writers of the era. He was also the most enduring—hence this series—and certainly among the most legendary. It all began only months after he first tried his hand at fiction, with L. Ron Hubbard tales appearing in *Thrilling Adventures, Argosy, Five-Novels Monthly, Detective Fiction Weekly, Top-Notch, Texas Ranger, War Birds, Western Stories,* even *Romantic Range.* He could write on any subject, in any genre, from jungle explorers to deep-sea divers, from G-men and gangsters, cowboys and flying aces to mountain climbers, hard-boiled detectives and spies. But he really began to shine when he turned his talent to science fiction and fantasy of which he authored nearly fifty novels or novelettes to forever change the shape of those genres.

Following in the tradition of such famed authors as Herman Melville, Mark Twain, Jack London and Ernest Hemingway, Ron Hubbard actually lived adventures that his own characters would have admired—as an ethnologist among primitive tribes, as prospector and engineer in hostile climes, as a captain of vessels on four oceans. He even wrote a series of articles for *Argosy*, called "Hell Job," in which he lived and told of the most dangerous professions a man could put his hand to.

Finally, and just for good measure, he was also an accomplished photographer, artist, filmmaker, musician and educator. But he was first and foremost a *writer*, and that's the L. Ron Hubbard we come to know through the pages of this volume.

This library of Stories from the Golden Age presents the best of L. Ron Hubbard's fiction from the heyday of storytelling, the Golden Age of the pulp magazines. In these eighty volumes, readers are treated to a full banquet of 153 stories, a kaleidoscope of tales representing every imaginable genre: science fiction, fantasy, western, mystery, thriller, horror, even romance—action of all kinds and in all places.

Because the pulps themselves were printed on such inexpensive paper with high acid content, issues were not meant to endure. As the years go by, the original issues of every pulp from *Argosy* through *Zeppelin Stories* continue crumbling into brittle, brown dust. This library preserves the L. Ron Hubbard tales from that era, presented with a distinctive look that brings back the nostalgic flavor of those times.

L. Ron Hubbard's Stories from the Golden Age has something for every taste, every reader. These tales will return you to a time when fiction was good clean entertainment and the most fun a kid could have on a rainy afternoon or the best thing an adult could enjoy after a long day at work.

Pick up a volume, and remember what reading is supposed to be all about. Remember curling up with a *great story*.

—Kevin J. Anderson

KEVIN J. ANDERSON *is the author of more than ninety critically acclaimed works of speculative fiction, including* The Saga of Seven Suns, *the continuation of the Dune Chronicles with Brian Herbert, and his* New York Times *bestselling novelization of L. Ron Hubbard's* Ai! Pedrito!

THE GREAT SECRET

THE GREAT SECRET

SWEEPING clouds shadowed the tawny plain, and far off in the east the plumes of night spread gently, mournfully, burying the corpse of the Livian day. Fanner Marston, a tattered speck upon a ridge, looked eastward, looked to the glory he sought and beheld it.

Throat and tongue swollen with thirst, green eyes blazing now with new ecstasy, he knew he had it. He would gain it, would realize that heady height upon which he had elected to stand. Before him lay the Great Secret! The Secret which had made a dead race rule the Universe! And that Secret would be his, Fanner Marston's, and Fanner Marston would be the ruler, the new ruler, the arbiter of destiny for all the Universe!

All through these weeks he had stumbled over the gutted plains toward these blue mountains beneath the scorching double sun. He had suffered agonies but he had won!

There, glittering in the yellow sunlight was Parva, dead, beautiful city of the ancients, city of the blessed, city of knowledge and power.

Fanner laughed. He was strong; he was lean; but he was not handsome; and of all the things about him this laugh, distorted by thirst-ravaged lips, was the least pleasant. His eyes, which had of late grown so very dull, flamed greenly with the ecstasy which came with that vision.

*There, glittering in the yellow sunlight was Parva, dead,
beautiful city of the ancients, city of the blessed,
city of knowledge and power.*

He had won. They had told him that he could not; the legends said it was not possible for any mortal man to win. But the spell of the ancients was broken, their books were open, their riches lay for the taking. Parva was there! Parva was his!

It mattered nothing to Fanner that nearly twenty miles of gashed and forbidding terrain still lay between him and his goal. It mattered not that his canteens were empty; nor did it matter that, behind the ridge on which he stood, his monocycle, last vehicle of his caravan, was a ruined wreck.

He was glad now that his companions were dead—of thirst, of quarrels, of disease. He would not have to murder the last of them now and so preserve to himself this incalculable thing which awaited him. Fate was shaping everything for him!

He could do these twenty miles by noon of the next day, do them the hard way, on foot and without water, for there was something to sustain him now; he knew that the city was real, had truly existed through all these ages, was just as the history books had said it was. And if this much was true, then all was true. And he had seen the silver river!

Fanner's boots were scuffed relics but he set forth down the rocky slope and so great was his ecstasy that he did not feel the sharp bites of the rocks, nor did he feel the fingers of thirst which were throttling him. He was hard; he could outlive forty men and had done it; he would succeed, for he was Fanner Marston!

He had fought these deserts and mountains and he had whipped them—almost. He would live through to the end, and see the Great Secret which awaited him emblazon his name throughout space!

Fanner Marston would bring a new era, a day when spaceships no longer had to land in seas to save themselves from being shattered, when men would be hampered no longer in combating the atmospheres of many now uninhabitable planets. The wealth of the Universe would be his for the taking; the entire race of mankind would bow to his command like vassals. For there, glittering in the sunset, was Parva—Parva, the city of the Great Secret.

Darkness caught him, and he groped his stumbling way among a great forest of black boulders. He did not mind the shocks of falling, the cuts inflicted upon him, the gouges of the unkind earth; nor did he mind the constantly increasing size of his tongue. Distance he had mastered; mere thirst would not stop him now. And besides, he had seen it, just like in the legends. The silver river. What cared he for thirst when that mighty stream awaited him?

Fanner Marston, master of the Universe: it was a pleasant title to resound through his brain.

Black-mouthed with thirst, stumbling with fatigue, lightheaded with his dream of power, he struggled on through the night.

Fanner Marston had always considered himself some favorite child of fate; he knew now that that must be so. How otherwise could he win through where so many had failed? How otherwise could he alone of forty men come to his goal? Fate meant this to happen to him; the devils who were his guardians strongly bore him to his victory. He alone would reach Parva; he alone would *know.*

He had forgotten where first he had heard the legends of this city he now approached, for he had not immediately grasped their truth and significance. As a child he had been too hardly driven as a slavey in a pirate camp to dream much on the mastery of the Universe. As a young man petty thievery in the large cities of the Universe had occupied his skills. Not until he had become master of his own craft and crew, not until he realized that there was destiny awaiting him, did he turn his mind in earnest upon Parva.

There, men said, lay the most advanced science of the Universe, sealed up in a strangely constructed city, covered with the dust of eons. It had been seen from afar by this one; it had been reported by a man gone mad with thirst; it had crept down the centuries in the literature of space. One and all agreed that Parva and Parva alone contained the sum total of knowledge gathered by a vanished race, one which had been so far advanced that ethereal communication with the planets had been possible, that its spaceships could land on ground. That civilization had used atomic power, not radioactive fuel. Its men had been able to clothe themselves against the rigors of the many uninhabitable planets. And then Parva alone remained of all that great culture and Parva itself had died. But within it there must be the Great Secret.

Of the Great Secret, men understood very little save that which had been expressed in a short formula. But with that formula a man might master *all.*

Fanner Marston had no qualms about getting out, for if he had the Great Secret, would not travel be a simple thing? He could see himself arriving in triumph on Earth, center of the universal culture which now obtained. He could hear the cheering throngs and feel the waves of adulation which would be his. And he could nearly taste the liquors—fantastically expensive and satisfying—which he would drink, and feel the warm flesh of the women who would love him, would love the master of the Universe. And he would tell men to go hither and thither; he would move great armies and fleets; he would cause vast conquests, and kings would bow before his brilliance and his might. For all of eternity he would be remembered. The Great Secret would be his.

Dreaming, not realizing how acutely his body suffered and how slender became his strength, he struggled on until dawn, through the dry washes, over the shaled ridges, through the gritty valleys. He to whom the most beautiful women and the most exquisite liquors of the Universe would be a commonplace could not be worried now about mere thirst and exhaustion.

As the light broke, and as he mounted a ridge, he could again see the city and before it the silver river. He had less than eight miles to go; the towers looked huge and overbearing. For a moment a small doubt clamored to be heard and then he swallowed it in a tidal wave of exultation. Women, liquor, power! He, Fanner Marston, stood on the threshold of All!

He started down the ridge, but fell and tumbled far before

he could stop himself and stand again. The physical shock of shale cutting into him as it slid brought him close to the reality which waited to torture him. His hand trembled as he sought to staunch a flow of blood from his thigh. A great weariness sought to sweep upward from that gash and with an angry gesture Fanner Marston put it down. He crossed the gully, clambered up the far side and went through the rocks toward the city. Now and then he stumbled, caught himself and stumbled again. Once he fell and lay sprawled for several minutes before consciousness returned.

It was the double sun, that's what it was. The great dumbbell star blazed furiously now, two hours into the day, and brought heat waves writhing up from the tawny plain, writhing up into the shrieking wind which raced clouds through the iridescent blue heavens. The avarice of that sun, which would let no moisture fall, took away what small stores of moisture might remain in Fanner Marston, took with them the hidden reserves of energy.

He fell more often now and the grin upon his swollen lips grew more fixed. Women, cheering throngs, liquor— he could think of them and find strength in them and go on. But little by little he was losing his grip upon the reality of his dreams and, gradually, he was becoming aware of the actuality of this searing plain, the shrieking, dry wind, the sharp rocks, the double sun which drained him and charred his very eyelids.

Crawling over the distance which remained, the single thought, water, obliterated his dreams for seconds at a time.

His tongue had begun to hold open his mouth. His throat was such that his breath came in strangling wheezes. Ah, damn it, he was earning the Great Secret. He was earning Parva. Only Fanner Marston would have nerve to go on. Another man would lie here, in the very sight of that river, would lie here and fry and die. Liquor . . . women . . . POWER! Liquor . . . women . . . power . . .

God, he was tired!

He lay still for a little while, shielding his eyes against the monstrous glare. And then he shook himself together and crawled painfully forward.

The double sun was in the zenith; the wind had increased in velocity until it picked up from the plains, as it had all the sand in the eons past, stones the size of baseballs and hurled them down again. Only the giant rocks themselves withstood that gale and the only surcease from its fury was close to their bases.

Water. He had to have water. He . . . had . . . to . . . have . . . God! Would that river never come close to him!

He did not realize that there was no river until he stood at the very base of the giant dome, holding to its polished base, staring up at the clear glass above. There was no silver river, there was only a silver fringe. No water.

But inside there would be water. Inside there would be the Great Secret which would solve all and with that there would be water!

He steadied himself. He must fall back upon these dreams.

These dreams alone would keep him going. Women. He had to think about women. Not water. Women. Women were the necessary things to his being. Liquor, he would think—

Water!

Damn you, he told himself, damn you, keep going. You can't quit now. I won't let you quit now. You are going through with this. You are going to become the master of the Universe. . . .

He crawled along the wall and found a port which opened easily to his touch. The sudden silence of the interior was a relief great enough to bring him strength again. Upright he stumbled down a silver street. It was cool in here after the fury of that double sun. Parva had been well planned. Something kept it cool even after these eons had passed. There were no signs of decay and these strangely built cubicles which flanked the streets stood as they had stood long ago.

Entering one he tried to find water. And he found none. He entered others, with no different result. A small panic began to grip him now which evaded his control. With the strange clarity pain sometimes brings, he knew that the river which had fed water to Parva had dried under the onslaught of the double sun. The pools which remained with their statuary in the street intersections were dry, dusty dry.

The Great Secret! The Great Secret which was almost within his reach would bring him water. It was reputed to bring everything, to be the key of anything. With controlled rationality he sought the mighty golden plaque which men said held the inscription. He knew he would find it. He knew the language in which it had been written and he had a dictionary of that language as the only possession he had brought through.

Water!

He steadied his nerves and sought calmly. His jaw ached with his swollen tongue and he could barely breathe. But he knew he would find the thing for which he sought. He was Fanner Marston. He was destined for greatness! Fanner Marston, ruler of the Universe! And what things would those riches buy!

The Great Secret had made this civilization great. And it would make the fame of Fanner Marston as great as eternity. He had won. He had only to look up. . . .

It hung in a room entered by four arched doors and the doors were open. Upon golden chains it dangled, that plaque, not even dulled by dust.

He sank to the floor, gazing at the inscription in ecstasy. His dreams flooded back upon him, revitalized him. He was not a broken and torn wretch crouching there, nearly dead with thirst and exhaustion, he was Fanner Marston at whose beck would come all those things for which he craved.

Scrawling upon the white, smooth floor, he began to decipher the words. He worked with nervous, impatient speed, reading nothing of what he wrote, saving until the last the full import of the Great Secret. He savored every instant of this work. Forgotten was his throat, his tongue, his gashed body.

And then he stared feverishly at the assembled words he had written and drank them in. He read again. Slowly, wearily, once more he read them.

The Great Secret that had made this civilization great . . .

If thou, O Man, would rule the worlds, the All,
First learn thou, the folly of matter and the material lusts.

SPACE CAN

SPACE CAN

LANCING through space, slammed along by a half million horses, the United States destroyer *Menace* anxiously sought the convoy which had been wailing to all the Universe for aid but now was still, still with an ominous quiet which could mean only its defeat.

She was only one, the *Menace*, and "they" would be more than one, but the little space can charged ahead, knowing well that she was a pebble from the mighty slingshot of the embattled fleet, a pebble where there should have been a shower of stones. Gracefully vicious, a bundle of frail ferocity, a wasp of space designed for and consecrated to the kill, the *Menace* flamed pugnaciously onward; she had her orders, she would carry them out to the last ounce of her fuel, the last charge in her guns and the last man within her complex and multiple compartments. She carried the Stars and Stripes upon her side, gold lace upon her bridge and infinite courage in her heart, for upon her belligerent little nose rested the full tradition of four-hundred-odd years of Navy, a tradition which took no dares, struck no colors and counted no odds.

She should have been a flotilla in this lonely cube of space, but with the fleet embattled off Saturn, no flotilla could be spared. She had done other jobs, hard ones, in this long war.

There was faith in her, too much perhaps, and so she was here alone, raking the black with her detectors, bristling with impatience to engage the enemy, be he cruiser or battleship or just another destroyer; she was a terrier who had no eyes for the size of her rats.

On her bridge a buzzer sawed into the roar of her motion, and her executive officer stood aside to permit her summoned captain a view of the detector. Her captain, Lieutenant Carter, steadied himself with a hand on Ensign Wayton's shoulder, and his face, usually young and efficient, became weary as he looked at the message which registered there.

In the detector, the supply ships were colorless spots, unmoving, without order. Among them were fainter dots which gruesomely indicated ships which were growing cool, having been emptied of air. Because spacesuits might mean desertion of crews near the first port, there were few in naval vessels unless they were crack ships like the *Menace*. This battle was almost over and there would be many, many dead.

One spot began to turn violet, which meant that a vessel, friend or foe, was heading toward the *Menace*.

Second-class Petty Officer Barnham was already training an analoscope on the red spot. He shuffled the spectrum plates of all navies until he had one which would compare with the lines on his screen.

"Saturn destroyer, sir," said Barnham matter-of-factly.

Lieutenant Carter shook himself into the fighting machine he was trained to be. The situation was a plain one, a simple one. The convoy had been set upon by a raiding fleet, the existence of which had not been suspected. Bravely the train's escorts had flashed into battle and had fought their ships to the last pound of air; that they had not done badly was indicated by the fact that only two Saturn vessels remained in action; that the entire escort was dead was plain in the silence of the battle communicator; that the supply ships were paralyzed and already half destroyed was to be found in the garble which spewed and gibbered from the all-channel speaker.

Another spot, which had evidently been traveling parallel to their course and so had showed white, now glowed dull red and Barnham said in a flat voice, "Another Saturn vessel, sir."

They were coming up now into action. They had perhaps thirty minutes of strain in store before the first searching blasts of flame came to them and their own guns began to seek the vitals of the enemy. The captain pushed a thumb down upon the battle-stations button and the clanging roar broke the tight lines which had invisibly stretched through the little destroyer.

It was a matter of seconds until Lieutenant Carter had his battle plan. Plainly, he wanted nothing to do with this first destroyer, for he could feel from across black space the eagerness of hope in it that he would attack it and disregard the second ship, while that vessel, with all the brutal efficiency of a thing which knows nothing but destruction, blasted the life from the remainder of the supply vessels.

Abruptly, Lieutenant Carter understood a thing which in his inevitable resentment at being detached from the great battle had escaped him, and he understood, too, that insufficient weight had been given to this mission. He should have been started early. He should have the rest of his flotilla in a comfortable V behind him. For now the detector gave out information in shape instead of light and disclosed that this supply train consisted of the majority of fuel vessels possessed by the Navy. Someone had blundered. Intelligence had failed to discover that an enemy raiding fleet had slipped away from Saturn; guard ships had blundered in letting it through; flag had erred by not suspecting the possibility. For in those big hulks was the blood of the fleet and without it victory or destruction were the only alternatives. The battle fleet, already far beyond its radius, had no reserve. And from the state of his own bunkers, Lieutenant Carter knew that no one had sufficient fuel to return to Earth!

Everywhere through the ship men were strapping themselves at their posts or donning the heavy padding which would protect them against the violent course changes which would throw the complement about like dice in a cup.

"Aloft ten, right rudder nineteen," said the captain.

The *Menace* leaped as the steering jets slammed her into her new course, as though she was unwilling to even countenance a thing which sought to avoid battle.

The screens of the enemy showed the action without much lag, and an instant later, the Saturn vessel was killing her speed on her old course and blasting into a new one which would again intercept the *Menace*.

The Saturnian, grudged Ensign Wayton, was well handled. Getting by her to engage the second was not going to be simple.

Lieutenant Carter leaned back in his deep command seat

and apparently lost interest in the whole thing, for there was a vague look in his eyes and a relaxed expression about his mouth. Seeing this, the quartermaster let out a small explosive sigh, for he knew that they would engage the first enemy.

Actually, the captain was examining the vast panel of meters which gave the small bridge the appearance of being set in diamonds and gold. When he saw that all guns were ready, that all tubes were firing, that the air pressure was even throughout the ship and the new tanks broached to give the men more energy and courage, he turned slightly to the blue-and-gold figure in the other wing and said quietly, "We will engage, Mr. Wayton."

Ensign Wayton's hands tensed over the panel above his knees and then fluttered for an instant as though he needed to test the buttons which would fire the batteries.

"Aye, aye, sir," said Ensign Wayton. He was breathing quickly, as though to supercharge his body with oxygen and hurl himself rather than flame projectiles at the enemy.

On the after bridge, before a similar but less complete board, Ensign Gates stood a lonely watch. He could look down the hatch just behind him and see the tense crew around the base of the Burmingham jet of the starboard engine. Ensign Gates swept his eyes back to the control panel, checked the telltales there and then glanced at his own quartermaster. The man, a heavyset sailor from Iowa, who still bore, after twenty years in space, the stamp of his state upon him, looked impersonally into the sphere compass which mirrored the stars and planets. He felt the officer's eyes on him and edged his appearance with a sharp professionalism, as though this

21

might communicate a greeting to the placid little ensign, of whom the quartermaster was fond in a shy, defiant way.

Ensign Gates grinned to himself, for he knew the meaning of the change in his quartermaster. He said something to the man, but the remark was engulfed in the crashing shudder of the port twenty-nines. They were engaged.

Time stood still and two vicious dots of ferocity slashed at each other in an immense black cube of vacuum. Shells burst like tiny flowers when they missed, or flashed like yellow charges of electricity when they struck. The *Menace* became filled with acridity. Somewhere in her a man was screaming an insane battle cry, and elsewhere blue blots of profanity hung thickly around guns and tubes and stoke ports.

Compartment 21 was holed and sealed from the rest of the ship between the beats of a chronometer. Compartment 16 turned into a blazing furnace and was sealed alike.

In the exact center of the ship, which was the after bridge, Ensign Gates placidly kept track of the enemy in the event that his firing panel had to take over. His active duty here was the overseeing of the engineering force, aft and below, but two tough chiefs were cursing themselves into a comfortable berth in Hades around the molten breeches of the tubes and needed no help.

"Hulled her!" barked the annunciator. Forward, Ensign Wayton sounded like a man cheering a baseball game rather than the director of that deadly blast. And then an instant later, "Hulled her!"

There was a crash topside and a man, bellowing agony and rage, hurled himself down a ladder. He was a mass of flames. The emergency squad member there smothered him swiftly in a blanket. Compartment 6 was sealed and everyone in her.

A small amount of Ensign Gates' placidity left his face. They were being severely knocked about by a vessel which had a longer range and a faster steering system, which was landing four hits to their two.

"Hulled her!" cried Ensign Wayton, an invisible source of death forward and above. Evidently something had happened to the Saturnian, for an instant later, in a steady stream, Wayton began to chant the *Menace*'s hits.

Examining the panel before him, Ensign Gates believed that a lucky shot had penetrated the steering jets of the enemy, for he was now traveling in a straight line through the remaining three vessels of the convoy as if to help out the other Saturnian in the convoy's destruction before this raging little wasp of space put an end to everyone. Just as the *Menace* flashed by a halted supply vessel, it bloomed into a sphere of scarlet death, the ammunition and highly explosive fuel igniting all at once.

Lieutenant Carter gazed calmly at the fleeing enemy, but the calmness was an official sort of thing, for there was sorrow for the supply ships and anger for the Saturnian snarled into a lump behind his gray eyes. Each time the *Menace* got a salvo home the captain twitched forward and a contraction of muscles above his mouth made him grin a split second at a time. His role was that of spectator so long as the ship was on her target, for then her steering was wholly between the gunnery officer and the helmsman.

With a blast close aboard, the Saturnian folded itself like a smashed tin can, and what had been an efficient fighting ship an instant before was now a scrap of volatilizing metal.

"Well done, Mr. Wayton," said Lieutenant Carter.

Ensign Wayton turned glowing eyes and battle-reddened cheeks upon his captain and didn't see him at all. He was already seeking the other Saturnian on his screen, was the gunnery officer, as though this first ship had merely served to calibrate his guns.

"Engage the second enemy, Mr. Wayton," said Lieutenant Carter.

The *Menace*, bristling and sure of herself, shot a streak of power from her starboard bow and stabbed into a new course, three quick jets on the port bow and one below settling her into this.

Telepathically, Lieutenant Carter was aware of his enemy's abrupt distaste for combat with him, now that the first Saturnian had been blasted from the action, but there was nothing in the action of the second vessel to indicate its dislike, for it turned now away from the supply vessel it had intended to spear, and streaked in a wide bank to bring her into a broadside parallel with the *Menace*.

Ensign Wayton adjusted his screen with the motor button and gave a swift check to the computator and then, because he was already ranged, sent all six guns of the port battery into a furious crescendo.

The *Menace,* dancing sideways from the recoils and being jabbed back by the adjusters, shivered with some vague premonition.

The Saturnian destroyer passed through the cone of concentration, sliding sideways to the *Menace* at a swift pace to throw off range and for some other purpose which was not to be fathomed for several seconds. The Saturnian's guns were winking bright spots and her flame wake, as it turned to white powdery smoke, curved and feathered. She was a well-built little vessel, a few feet longer than the *Menace* and thicker through.

Lieutenant Carter scanned space with his detector but found no sign of reinforcement for the remaining destroyer.

The *Menace* shivered as she was knocked off course. The check board blinked and Compartment 26 vanished from it. Then, in terrifyingly swift order, the lights indicating Compartments 27, 28, 29 and 30 went black.

An annunciator above the captain's post said in a calm voice, "Starboard magazine gone. Fire spreading."

The quartermaster's eyes flicked to the captain. Ensign Wayton hesitated for an instant over his firing buttons and then his gold stripe flashed as he located and aimed all three space torpedoes on the starboard. He launched them and said in a tightly casual voice to the quartermaster, "Roll a hundred and eighty." Ensign Wayton, having no starboard batteries, was in action with the port.

Compartments 31, 25 and 36 went out in order. The air in the ship was unbreathable.

"Spacesuits," said Lieutenant Carter into the annunciator. "All hands."

The space torpedoes were sped, but only one had struck—this in the after section of the Saturnian, where it had caused a vast fan of bright fireworks. It had wiped out the stern balancing jets, but that vessel's main propulsions were apparently without harm.

A new crash shook the *Menace* and the big light which marked the after bridge went black.

There was the smallest hint of concern in Lieutenant Carter's voice. "Mr. Gates!"

Silence answered.

With steel bands on his nerves, his voice carefully steady, Lieutenant Carter said, "Mr. Gates. Please report."

There was silence which hung for a heartbeat throughout the entire vessel.

Dead white, Ensign Wayton glanced at his captain. It was an appeal of dependence, shot without thought, an agonized hope that something could be done, a last belief in the impossibility that anything could ever happen to placid, easy Ensign Gates.

Lieutenant Carter did not look at his executive officer. In a flat, official voice he said, "Grapple the enemy."

The heat was so intense in the dying *Menace* that men felt it through their spacesuits. They were unwilling to begin upon their private stores of oxygen until smoke was too thick in the hull to be breathed. Now they were in communication with helmet phones.

Space-garbed, a relief came to the quartermaster to allow him to climb into his suit. He had been standing there, strangling and sweating at the helm, and he would have stood there until he had melted if his relief had not come. The captain took the firing panel while Ensign Wayton slid into his suit. And then Lieutenant Carter dropped into his own ready covering. The captain gasped with relief as he sucked in air.

There was a clatter in the phones as arms were being issued out. Though the batteries were firing still, the helmet cut down their roaring to a tremble, which one felt with his body. There was something ominous and horrible in this silence for every man on the ship, for each was affected alike in the connection of the silence to a sudden surge of loneliness. For perhaps three minutes there was irregularity in the smoothness of the execution of duties, and then the first shock of quiet wore away and men began to talk to each other on the individual battery frequencies, began to swear anew, began to revile and damn this enemy who was destroying the sleek little *Menace*.

Still firing, Ensign Wayton was adjusting his ranges so as to sweep them in closer and closer to the attacking ship. The Saturnian was suffused with superiority and satisfaction, for the burning wake of the *Menace* was plainly visible as were the gaping holes in her skin, and this feeling, knowing it existed, Lieutenant Carter utilized by ordering unsteady leaps and veering as though the vessel were not quite under complete control.

Confident and disdainful, the Saturnian welcomed the closing. She even swept to starboard, little by little, to aid the action. It was her belief that gunnery was the only concern of the *Menace* and this, from a blasted vessel with only two guns still going, she could amply risk.

Further punishment awaited the Navy ship, for she could not come so close without being struck repeatedly. Her bow vanished to within twenty feet of the bridge and she was steering now with her guns alone, having two amidships port and one forward starboard, as well as her one-inch batteries on the bridge itself. She was rolling, tortured, nearly out of control, darting up and back and even tumbling when she came within a quarter of a mile of the Saturnian. And then what happened was swiftly done. The grapnels were still in action as they had been designed to be, and the one last ace of the gallant little vessel was played.

With a shuddering stab which tightened and held, the invisible claws of the *Menace* fastened upon the Saturnian and sucked them together with a swiftness which could only end in a numbing crash.

The shock of collision further crumpled the nose and drove a deep bulge into the side of the Saturnian. The latter had been panicked upon the instant of realization that something was amiss and had sought to charge away into space and get free, momentarily forgetful that she still possessed a superior force of men. But now that the adhesion was achieved, she ceased blasting and prepared for the fury which would come—which was already on its way.

Disintegrators in the hands of a burly CPO and his gang ate a hole into the Saturnian at the point of contact as though that hull consisted of cheese.

There was no more on the bridge for Lieutenant Carter. Here his responsibility was done. Ensign Wayton was already gone from the panel and the quartermaster, a huge machete he favored in close quarters gripped competently in his hand, was just vanishing through the hatch.

"Boarders away!" the captain barked at the annunciator in his helmet. He was through the hatch before the yell had ceased to beat against his own ears.

Ahead he saw a knot of men launching itself against another knot which barred the ragged circle of emptiness that led into the Saturnian. Flame was spitting back into the boarders from viciously wielded jets and here and there a spacesuit was giving way to the heat. And then Carter threw himself through the group, jet pistol in hand, and torpedoed himself into the mob just within the Saturnian. With a howl of approval, the sailors followed their captain.

The mass in which he found himself cut at him, shot at him, grabbed at him, and Carter, spinning around and around and firing a space clear, yelled defiantly but incoherently at them.

For several seconds the captain did not realize that the Saturnians had been too contemptuous to don spacesuits—if they had them—for, at best, it was difficult to use them at the guns. It had never occurred to the enemy destroyer that

Disintegrators in the hands of a burly CPO and his gang
ate a hole into the Saturnian at the point of contact
as though that hull consisted of cheese.

a thing as mad as a boarding would be attempted by such a mauled ship, particularly since the odds in men against such a ship would be three to one.

The curiously pointed heads of the repelling sailors ducked back from the fury of the pistol and then the mass swept deeper into the ship, evidently in receipt of an order which was calculated to draw the invaders into passageways where fast-firing small arms could be brought into play upon them.

Swirling about their captain, the seamen of the *Menace* cut down the stragglers and slipped in their blood. Few guns were here, for the sailors uniformly preferred steel when close quarters were to be had.

Suddenly the front rank of the invaders was swept back, driving their followers to cover. Two of the bodies were dead and projectiled toward the *Menace* by the fury of the fire they had met.

Ensign Wayton, a furiously moving monster in his spacesuit, shot to their fore, insane for an instant in the belief that his captain had been killed. When he saw Lieutenant Carter, he stopped screaming into his helmet. He halted.

"Spread into cover," said Carter quickly. "Try to filter up into the ship through those hatches. But don't press them closely and don't risk your men."

"Aye, aye, sir," said Ensign Wayton. He spent no time in wondering why his captain went back through the crowd, for he had received his orders and he would carry them out to the last word and with his last breath. He looked around him at the shining walls of the gun room in which they had arrived and crisply told off a chief petty officer to burn out a section of its wall. If the passages were covered, there would be other ways of getting through the ship. He had an instant's wonder about their fate, for he knew very well that this handful, less than twenty—less than fifteen, he saw with a shock—were pitted against at least fifty well armed in their own ship.

"Lively, now," said Ensign Wayton.

As captain, Lieutenant Carter had no questions to answer or reasons to give. He was glad of that. He had a competent officer in Ensign Wayton, who knew what to do if anything happened to his commander. And this was a job Lieutenant Carter could not relegate to anyone.

He faltered for an instant on the threshold of the burning *Menace*. It was not the heat which repelled him so much as the unwillingness to see again this dying little vessel which had been, until such a short time before, a well-ordered, shipshape example of what a United States Navy destroyer should be. Here, for two years, he had gone through the routines, the problems and the alternating bursts of good and bad news which had marked this campaign. He had been one with an alive, sensitive creature of steel and chromium and flame, and to enter her now was like walking upon the corpse of one's friend. He had a feeling that she should be left alone, as she was, to die, still facing the enemy.

Lieutenant Carter stepped over the jagged sill of the hole which had been carved in the Saturnian. The need of haste was upon him now, both because the possibility of his getting through the flames before him required speed and because this was a hideous job, the better to be done quickly.

The first blast struck him when a gun charge fired somewhere on the deck nearby. He was catapulted against the steel bulkhead and stood there for an instant in the swirling yellow gloom, shaking his head and trying to recall what he was about. Anxiously, he gripped at the elusive facts, for he was badly stunned. Then, with clearing sight, he sped aft and up through the curling tongues which had already stripped the paint from the walls.

There was no resemblance to the trim little *Menace* in this twisted, blackened mess through which he drove himself. He tried to think there was not. He knew there was.

He fumbled in his bag for a grenade as he lurched through the painful fog and when he had it in his thick glove, it required much of his nerve to keep it with him, for tongues of fire were reaching at it, heating it.

He found the ladder to the engine room. The grease had burned away, and because it was hot, his shoes stuck tenaciously to the rungs as though the *Menace*, lonely, was trying for the company of her master in a last shiver of her death throes.

Lieutenant Carter could feel a throb which did not come from flames. He worked toward it. He seemed to be taking forever for this task. The air in his tank was already scalding his lungs. The ship's oxygen tanks must be feeding these flames, and if that were so, then they might explode at any instant. They were close above him now.

He found the generators, still running furiously in all this heat, fed by the treble-protected batteries which made a boarding possible after a ship was in ruins. He hauled a plate from the first layer of armor and then groped through the second and third. That he tried to pull the pin of the grenade with his teeth recalled him into a calm and orderly chain of thought. He plucked at the pin with his glove-thick fingers and got it out. He dropped it upon the batteries and in the same motion spun about and staggered toward the ladder. The heat inside his suit was so intense now that he had to will himself to breathe, and each time he did he flinched as he felt his lungs shrink away.

He clawed through a hatch and scrambled down a passageway. Blind and groping, he found the door in the yellow smoke and stumbled through.

The jagged hole in the side of the Saturnian was just ahead of him, he knew. He could not see it. He sought along the plates with anxious fingers.

Abruptly, he was tumbling forward, breath knocked out of him by another exploding charge. Dazedly, he lifted his helmeted head.

There was a great sighing rush of smoke and fire and a mighty hand snatched him from the deck and slammed him against plates. Groggily, he fought again to rise and then fought even harder, for it would have been very comforting to slump and go out, with the hands of his sailors supporting him.

The smoke of the *Menace* had filled this compartment of the Saturnian. But there was no smoke here now. And there was no air. The empty vacuum was greedy and swelled out the spacesuits to their normal proportions. Where the *Menace* had been, there was now only a gaping black hole. Once her generators, which kept the grapnels alive, had been shorted

out, the furious efforts of upper gunners in the Saturnian had
at last succeeded in blowing her away from the side.

Ensign Wayton was grinning through his transparent helmet
when he had at last ascertained that his captain was safe and
not seriously hurt.

Through the phones, Ensign Wayton said, "Sir, we have
carved our way through the bulkheads into their after bridge.
We have lost but three men. Your orders?"

"Yes," said Lieutenant Carter. "Yes, of course." He shook
his head vigorously to clear it. "Well done, Mr. Wayton."
Then thought took over from mechanical form and with a
glad surge he gripped his officer by the shoulder. "Quick!
Open their compartments! Open their compartments!"

The idea flooded in upon Ensign Wayton. It was less than
twenty feet up to the hole their jets had carved into the bridge
deck. The one dead sailor from the *Menace* and the officer
and two quartermasters of the Saturnian were bloated, even
exploded, into no semblance of humanity or Saturnity. The
CPO, who held the fort there belligerently, cut away at the
bulkhead with his jet and suddenly a great gust of air and
equipment shot him back.

Ensign Wayton steadied himself at the compartment board
and began to open the switches. Some of them were frozen
and he realized that the master panel was on the forward
bridge. The compartments went shut and their lights began to
go out. An officer up there was thinking fast. Ensign Wayton
thought faster. He snatched at the auxiliary voice tube caps
and yanked them. Into the holes he poured a dozen flame

shots. A scream of air, loud enough to penetrate the thick space helmets, greeted his action. The hurricane which came through the voice tubes from the forward bridge knocked him backward. The master panel had been cut in. Suddenly all panel lights glowed on the auxiliary board as lack of air pressure on the forward bridge threw control aft. With swift hands, Ensign Wayton switched the compartments open throughout the ship and a shuddering wail went through the vessel, every plate trembling as the life poured from her. Those suits, denied the Saturnians to ensure their fighting to the last compartment, had cost her, finally and forever, her crew.

Lieutenant Carter, beside his officer, spoke on the general-order frequency of his helmet. "Attention. Proceed carefully through the vessel and clean out anyone left in her." He turned to Ensign Wayton. "Take over, Mr. Wayton."

Seating himself at the communicator, Lieutenant Carter's eyes were vague with thoughtfulness. Absently, he commented that Washington's onetime predilection for trading patents was not without benefit, for this communicator panel might have borne the stamp of Bell Radiophone for its similarity.

He knew he should feel jubilant, knew that he should savor this report to the battle fleet, knew that victory and triumph were personally his. But, somehow, he had ashes on his tongue and the words he tried to arrange in his mind were dull, gray things.

He was thinking now of the *Menace*. In the letdown which had followed this battle, he knew he would think of her more and more. Proud, arrogant little space can, smashed by the insensate hates of a space war, drifting a derelict, a battered sacrifice to her pride, a dead cold thing lost in the immensity, to be shunned by all vessels who sighted her as a navigational risk.

There was victory but there was no victory. He could not think of a proper report, one which would measure up to the little scrap of history they had made. This story would be told in wardrooms for many years, how the little space can took on two larger than she, how she had saved the supply vessels of the battle fleet and how she had died in the saving. Lieutenant Carter could not see the panel clearly and was annoyed with himself. He flung away from it and the reports which were coming to him now concerning the state of the Saturnian, reports which were good, had only a routine meaning. They reached his ears, his official mind, but they went no deeper.

There was a slight jar through the ship, a thing which required no explanation but which seemed to herald something electric. Lieutenant Carter glanced about him. He swung down the ladder to the lower gun room and glanced questioningly at the sentry stationed by the jagged hole in the Saturnian's hull.

And then Carter froze.

For the hole was no longer empty! Had he dreamed that he got the *Menace* away from there? Had it been possible that she would not have herself abandoned?

There she was, the *Menace*! With her shattered bow pushed up into position and the fire-scarred depths of her clear of flame, she bumped gently against her conquered enemy.

And as Lieutenant Carter stared, he saw a man in a spacesuit moving toward him out of the shattered ship, followed by yet another.

Lieutenant Carter started and then quickly composed himself by pushing away the surge of elation which coursed through him.

The man in the spacesuit saluted. "Ensign Gates, sir. Fire shorted our conduits and cut us off. As soon as we dressed and opened the after bridge, we had things under control there. When the air went out of her hull, the fires stopped. She isn't in such bad shape, sir. Your orders?"

Lieutenant Carter saw through a strange mistiness and carefully pitched his voice for calmness. "Very good, Mr. Gates. You will take charge of the repair parties as soon as we get air back into these ships." He returned his engineering officer's salute with unusual smartness.

Gently, the little *Menace* nudged her battered nose against the hull of her conquered enemy as though to remind the Saturnian that a ship, even when shot half to hell, should never be considered in any light save that of a dangerous adversary. For an instant Carter was startled into a belief that the *Menace* was laughing, and then he saw that the sound issued from his phones and was sourced aloft where Gates and Wayton were gladly greeting each other. It amused him to think that his ship could laugh, for the fact was most ridiculous. Or was it?—he asked himself suddenly. Or was it?

THE BEAST

THE BEAST

THE crash and the scream which reverberated through the stinking gloom of the Venusian night brought Ginger Cranston to a startled halt upon the trail, held there for an instant by the swirl of panicked blues which made up the safari of the white hunter.

Something had happened to the head of the line, something sudden, inexplicable in this foggy blackness.

Ginger Cranston did not long remain motionless, for the blues had dumped their packages and had vanished, leaving the narrow trail, which wandered aimlessly through the giant trees, clear of men.

He took one step forward, gun balanced at ready in the crook of his arm, and then the thing happened to him which would make his life a nightmare.

From above and behind something struck him, struck him with a fury and a savageness which sent him flat into the muck, which began to claw and rake and beat at him with a singleness of intent which would have no ending short of death.

The white hunter rolled in the slime and beat back with futile fists, kicking out with his heavy boots, smothering under the gagging odor of a wild animal, so strong that it penetrated through the filters of his swamp mask, the only thing which was saving his face from the sabers this thing had for claws.

Fighting it back, the hunter's hands could find no grip upon the slimy fur; he could see nothing of it because of the dark and the fact that the blues had dropped their torches to a man. Ginger luridly cursed the blues, cursed this thing, cursed the muck and the agony which was being hammered into him.

He lurched to his knees, striking out blindly with all his might. The thing was driven back from him for an instant and Ginger's hands raked the mud around him for some weapon, preferably his lost gun. When he could not find it he leaped all the way to his feet and ripped away the swamp mask. He could not see. He could hear the snarling grunts of the thing as it gathered itself for a second charge.

Something in the unexpectedness of the attack, something in the ferocity of the beast, shook Ginger's courage, a courage which was a byword where hunters gathered. For a moment he could think of nothing but trying to escape this death which would again be upon him in an instant. He whirled and fumbled his way through the trees. If he could find some place where he could make a stand, if he could grasp a precious instant to get out and unclasp his knife—

There was a roaring sound hard by, the sound of battered water. Ginger knew this continent better than to go so far off a trail and he knew he must here make that stand. He gathered his courage about him like armor. He unclasped the knife. He could feel the beast not two yards away from him, but in the dense gloom he could not see anything but the vague shapes of trees.

It struck. It struck from behind with a strength which brought them crashing into the mud and branches. One cruel paw was crooked to feel out with its sabers the eyes of its victim, the others scored Ginger's back and side.

Rolling in a red agony, strong beyond any past strength, Ginger tried to slam his assailant back against a tree. He could not grip the slimy, elusive paw but he could brace it away from him with his forearm.

A roaring sound was loud in Ginger's ears and before he could halt the last roll he had managed, beast and hunter were over the lip and into black and greedy space. A shattering cry came from the beast as it fell away.

Ginger tried to see, tried to twist in the air and then he was gagged by the thick syrup of the depths and twisted like a chip in the strength of a whirlpool. He struck upward and then could not orient himself. His lungs began to burn and the syrup of the river seared his throat. The whirlpool flung him out, battered him against a rock and then left him to crawl, stunned and aching, from the stream.

He lay on the rocks, deafened by the roar of the water, trying to find strength enough to scan the space around him in search of the beast.

Two hours later the frightened blues, grouped in a hollow ring for security, found the white hunter by the river and placed him in a sling. One of the trackers nervously examined a nearby track and then cried, "*Da juju! Da juju!*" Hastily the carriers lifted the sling and bore its inert burden back to the trail and along it to the village which had been Ginger Cranston's goal.

Ginger Cranston woke slowly into the oppressive odor of a blue village from the tangled terror of his dreams. The heated ink of the Venusian night eddied through his tent, clung clammily to his face, smothered the native fires which burned across the clearing. Ginger Cranston woke into a new sensation, a feeling of loss, and for a little while could not bring organization into thought. It was hard for him to bring back the successive shocks which had placed him here, helpless in this bed, and he began to know things which it had never before occurred to him that it would be important to know.

He had always been a brave man. As government hunter of this continent, relentlessly wiping out the ponderous and stupid game which threatened the settlements and their crops, he had been considered all about as a man without peer in the lists of courage. So certain had he been in his possession of this confidence that he had never wondered about fear, had found only contempt for those who were so weak as to feel that lowly emotion.

And now Ginger Cranston woke up afraid.

The shocks, wreaked upon another, would have brought madness. To have been struck twice from behind by a raging beast, to have tasted death between the claws of such fury, would have wrecked the usual nervous system. But Ginger Cranston was not a usual person and, never having been other than his gay, confident self, he had no standards.

He had lost his courage.

In its place was a sick nausea.

And Ginger Cranston, out of shame, was no help to himself but stood away from his battered body and gazed with lip-curled contempt upon this sniveling hulk, which shook at the brink of recalling that which had brought this about. He had no sympathy for himself and had no reasons with which to excuse his state.

He was ill and his spirits, as in anyone ill, were low. He had been expecting the same stupid, many-tonned brutes which he had thought to constitute the only game of this continent. He had been set upon by a thing wholly unknown to him at a time when he had expected nothing and he had been mauled badly in the process. But he offered himself none of these. He was afraid, afraid of an unknown, cunning something, the memory of which was real in this dark tent.

"Ambu!" he yelled.

A Venusian of wary step and worried eyes slunk into the tent. Ambu had done his bungling best with these wounds, hurling the offer of help back into the teeth of the village doctor—a person who preferred a ghost rattle to a bottle of iodine. Ambu was of uncertain age, uncertain bearing. He was half in and half out of two worlds—that of the whites in Yorkville on the coast, that of the blues in the somber depths of this continent. He believed in ghosts. But he knew that iodine prevented infection. He belonged to a white, had been indifferently schooled by the whites. But he was a blue.

Ambu hung the lantern on the pole of the tent and looked uneasily at his white man. He was not encouraged by that strange expression in the hunter's eyes, but the fact that Lord Ginger had come back to consciousness was cheering.

Ginger was feeling a strange relief at having light. He smiled unconvincingly. When he spoke his voice was carefully controlled.

"Well, Ambu! I'm not dead yet, you see."

"Ambu is very happy, Lord Ginger." He looked worried.

"What . . . er . . . what happened out there when . . . well, what happened?" said Ginger with another smile.

Ambu looked into the dark corners of the tent, looked out into the compound and then sank on his dull haunches at the side of the cot.

"Devils," said Ambu.

"Nonsense," said Ginger in careful carelessness.

"Devils," said Ambu. "There was a pit. I have never before seen such a pit. It was dug deep with claw marks on the digging. It was covered over with branches and mud like a roof; when the trackers stepped upon it they fell through. There were sharpened stakes at the bottom to receive them. They do not live, Lord Ginger."

"A deadfall?" gaped Ginger. And then, because there was a resulting emotion which clamored to be felt, he spoke swiftly, carelessly, and smothered it. "Nonsense. There's nothing like a deadfall in the arts of the blues. There have been no hostile blues for thirty years or more."

"Devils," said Ambu. "Devils of the dark, not blues. I have never seen nor heard of such a trap, Lord Ginger."

"I'll have to see it before I believe it," said Ginger. "Er . . . Ambu, bring me a drink."

Ambu was perceptive. He knew Lord Ginger did not mean water even though Lord Ginger never drank except to be polite or when ill with fever. He poured from a flat metal bottle into a metal cup and the two chattered together.

"Very cold tonight," said Ambu, sweating.

"Very cold," said Ginger, drinking quickly.

The beasts of this continent weighed many tons. They were of many kinds, some of them carnivorous, all of them stupid, slothful swamp creatures which did damage because they were clumsy, not because they were vicious. It was a government hunter's job to kill them because a man had to be skilled to rend apart enough flesh and muscle and bone to keep the brutes from traveling. There were no small animals like leopards or lynxes. On all Venus there was nothing which weighed four hundred pounds and had claws, was cloaked in slimy fur—

"It *knew*," said Ambu. "It knew Lord Ginger would stop in just that place when the line halted. And it was on a tree limb above Lord Ginger waiting for him to stop. It *knew*."

"Rot and nonsense," grinned Ginger carefully. "I have never heard of a beast with that much intelligence."

"No beast," said Ambu with rare conviction for him. "Probably devil. No doubt devil. Forest devil. Drink again, Lord Ginger?"

Ginger drank again and some of the numb horror began to retreat before the warmth of the liquor. "Well, maybe we'll take a crack at hunting it when we've disposed of this *juju* thing the village is troubled about."

"The devil is *da juju*," said Ambu. "That is the thing for which they wanted Lord Ginger. That was *da juju*!"

"The white lord is well?" said a new voice, a tired and hopeless voice, in the entrance to the tent.

Ambu started up guiltily and began to protest to the chief in blue that the white lord was well enough but would talk to no one.

"Never mind, Ambu. Invite him in," said Ginger. He knew he would get the full impact of this thing now, would remember all about it, would receive the hopelessness of this gloomy forest chief like one receives an immersion in ink. "Greetings," said Ginger in blue.

"Greetings to the white lord," said the chief tiredly. "He lives and the village Tohyvo is happy that he lives. The white hunter is great and his fame is mighty. He comes and all things flee in horror before him. The blues beat their heads against the earth in submission and hide their eyes before the dazzling brilliance of the mighty lord." He sighed and sank upon an ammunition box.

"Greetings to the star of his people," said Ginger, mechanically. "His name carries the storms of his wrath across the jungle and his power is as the raging torrent. A flash of his glance is the lightning across the storm." He took a cup of liquor from Ambu and handed it to the dispirited, sodden little chief.

"You met *da juju*," said the chief.

"We did," said Ginger with a tired smile. "On the next meeting *da juju* will be dead."

"Ah," said the chief.

"You have had some trouble with this thing?" said Ginger.

"My best warriors are gutted and mangled corpses in the

forest depths. Women going to the river have never returned. Children are snatched from play. And always the dark swallows this thing, always there is only the silent forest to mock. In my long life I have never heard of such a beast. But you have said it will be killed. It is good. It is ended. The mighty hunter gives me back my sleep."

"Wait," said Ginger. "You say it makes raids on your village?"

"Yes, mighty warrior."

"How does it do this?"

"It rides down from the sky. It vanishes back into the sky."

"You mean the trees," said Ginger.

"It is the same," sighed the chief, eyeing the liquor bottle.

"How do your warriors die?"

The chief squirmed. "They fall into pits cunningly placed on the trail and covered over. They are attacked from behind and torn to bits. *Da juju* has even been known to wrest from their hands their spears and knives and transfix them with their own weapons."

Ambu was shivering. He stood on one foot, then on the other. He scratched his back nervously and in the next second scratched his head. His eyes, flicking back and forth from the chief to the white hunter, were like a prisoner's under torture.

"Maybe devils," said Ambu.

"Devils," muttered the old chief. "The mighty white warrior has come. All will be well. All will be well." He looked dispiritedly at Ginger and crept out of the tent.

Ambu pointed to a case which contained a radiophone. "Lord Ginger talk Yorkville and ask for men?"

Ginger startled himself by almost agreeing. He had never

asked for help. He was Ginger Cranston. He looked at the radio case like a desert-stranded man might gaze thirstily at a cup of water before he did the incredible thing of pouring it out on the ground.

"We won't need any help," said Ginger with a smile. "All I need is a night's sleep. Have the chief throw out beaters in the morning and pick up the beast's track. Meantime, good night. NO!" he added quickly and then calmed his voice. "No, leave the lantern there, Ambu. I . . . I have some notes to make."

Ambu looked uncertainly at his white master and then sidled from the tent.

The giant trees stood an infinity into the sky, tops lost in the gray dark of swirling vapors. Great tendrils of fog crept ghostily, low past the trunks, to blot with their evil odor of sulphur and rot what visibility the faint light might have permitted. It was an atmosphere in which men unconsciously speak in whispers and look cautiously around each bend before venturing farther along the trail.

The beaters had come back with news that *da juju* had left tracks in a clearing two kilometers from the village and they added to it the usual blue exaggeration that it was certain *da juju* was wounded from his encounter with the mighty white hunter.

The party stepped cautiously past an open space where some wrecked and forgotten space liner, which furnished the natives with metal, showed a series of battered ports through the swirling gloom, a ship to be avoided since its dryness offered refuge to snakes.

Weak and feverish, Ginger occasionally stopped and leaned against a tree. He would have liked the help of Ambu's arm, but could not, in his present agitated state, bring himself to ask for it.

Step by step, turn by turn of the trail, a thing was growing inside Ginger Cranston, a thing which was like a lash upon his nerves. His back was slashed with the wounds he had received and the wounds burned, burned with memory.

His back was cringing away from the thing it had experienced and as the minutes went the feeling increased. At each or any instant he expected to have upon him once again the shock of attack, from behind, fraught with agony and terror. He tried to sweep it from him. He tried to reassure himself by inspecting the low-hanging limbs under which they passed; but the memory was there. He told himself that if it did happen he would not scream. He would whirl and begin to shoot. He would smash the thing against a tree trunk and shatter it with flame and copper.

He was being careful to discount any tendency toward weakness and when, on a halt, he had found that each time he had pressed his back solidly against a tree, he thereafter turned his back to the trail and faced the tree.

Ambu was worried. He padded beside Lord Ginger, carrying the spare gun, wanting to offer his help, wanting to somehow comfort this huge man who was now so changed.

"Hot, eh?" said Ginger with a smile.

"Hot," said Ambu.

"Ask the trackers if we are almost there."

Ambu chattered to the men ahead and then shrugged. "They say a little way now."

"Good," said Ginger, carefully careless.

The trail began to widen and the river of syrup which ran in it began to shoal. The clearing was about them before they could see that it was and then the only sign was a certain lightness to the fog.

"Tracks!" cried the blue in advance.

Ginger went up to him. He wiped his face beneath his swamp mask and put the handkerchief carefully away. He knelt casually, taking care that his thigh boots did not ship mud and water over their tops. Impersonally he regarded the tracks.

There were six of them in sets of two. The first were clearly claws; two and a half feet behind them the second set showed no claws; two and a half feet back from these the third and last set showed claws again. The weight of the thing must be less than three hundred pounds.

A prickle of knowing went up the back of Ginger's spine. These tracks were perfect. They had been placed in a spot where they would retain their impressions. And from here they led away into the trees; but to this place they did not exist.

"Devil," chattered Ambu.

A devil was very nearly an acceptable explanation to Ginger. No six-tracked animal was known to him, either on this planet or any other.

Suddenly he stood up, no longer able to bear the feeling of attack from behind. He turned slowly. The dark vapors curled and drifted like veils through the clearing.

"Get on the track of it," said Ginger in blue.

The trackers trotted out, too swiftly for Ginger to keep up without extreme effort, but Ginger made no protest.

He told himself that the fever made him this way, but he had had fever before. Deep within he knew that the beast had a thing which belonged to Ginger, a thing which Ginger had never imagined could be stolen. And until he met that beast and killed that beast, he would not recover his own.

The tracks led on a broad way, clear in the mud, with a straight course. Uneasily, Ginger watched behind him, recalling the words of the chief that the thing often backtracked. But there were no overhanging branches in this part and that gave some relief, for they had come up a gradual grade and the trail was flanked with tall, limber trees which barred no light. Here the ground was more solid even if covered with thick masses of rot and the combination of greater light and better footing caused a weight to gradually lift from Ginger's back.

And then it happened. There was a swishing, swooping sound and a scream from Ambu! Ginger spun about to scan the backtrail—and to find nothing. Ambu was gone.

Ginger looked up. In a cunningly manufactured sling, not unlike a rabbit snare, held by one foot, was Ambu, thirty feet from the ground, obviously dead, his head smashed in from its contact with the trunk of the tree which, springing upright, had lifted him.

After a few moments Ginger said in a controlled voice, "Cut him down."

And some hours later the group crawled back into the compound, carrying Ambu, Ginger still walking by himself despite the grayness of his face and the strange tightness about his mouth.

With each passing day the lines on Ginger Cranston's face deepened and the hollows beneath his eyes grew darker. It was harder now to bring a proper note of cheerfulness into his commands, to reassure when all chances of success diminished with each casualty to the hunting party.

There came, one dull drab day, the final break with the blues. Ginger Cranston had seen it coming, had known that his own power had grown less and less in their eyes, that their faith in the great white hunter had slimmed to a hopeless dejection. *Da juju* had sapped the bulwark of morale and now the battlement came sliding down like a bank of soupy Venusian mud. Ginger Cranston woke to empty tents. The villagers said nothing, for there was nothing to say. The great white hunter was defeated. It was inevitable that the remainder of his crew would desert and it was not necessary that the way of their going be told, for the blazing mouths of guns could not have driven them back. Seven had died. Five remained to flee and the five had fled.

"Bring me trackers," said the haggard white man.

The chief looked at the mud and regarded it with intensity. He looked at a *pegunt* rooting there as though he had seen such an animal for the first time. He looked at a tree with searching interest.

"I said trackers!" said Ginger Cranston.

The chief scratched himself and began to sidle away, still without meeting the eyes of the white man.

Ginger struck out and the chief crumpled into a muddy, moaning pile.

"TRACKERS!" said Ginger.

The chief turned his face into the slime and whimpered. In all the village not one blue could be observed, but one felt that all the village had seen and now dispiritedly sank into a dull apathy as though this act of brutality, borne out of temper, was not a thing to be blamed but merely a thing which proved that the great white hunter was no longer great. With all the rest, *da juju* had him, had his heart and soul, which was far worse than merely having his life.

Ginger turned away, ashamed and shaken. He pushed his way into his tent and mechanically wiped the rain from his face, discovering abruptly that he wept. He could not now gain back the thing which *da juju* had. His means were gone with his men. He could hear the chief whimpering out there in the mud, could hear a wind in the great trees all around the place, mixed with the toneless mutter of the drizzle upon the canvas.

In the metal mirror which hung on the pole, steamed though it was, Ginger caught a glimpse of his countenance. He started, for that which he saw was not in the least Ginger Cranston; it was as though even the bone structure had somehow shifted to complete another identity. He had no impulse to strike the mirror down—he was tired, achingly, horribly tired. He wanted to crawl into his bed and lie there with his face to the blank wall of canvas and never move again.

Shame was the only active emotion now, shame for the

thing he had done just now, for the chief hardly came to his shoulder and the mud-colored body was twisted by accident and illness into a caricature of a blue. Ginger took a bottle from a case and went out again into the rain.

He knelt beside the chief and sought to turn him over and make him look. But the resistless shoulder was a thing which could not be turned and the low, moaning whimper was not a thing which would stop.

"I am sorry," said Ginger.

But there was no change. Ginger set the bottle down in the mud beside the head and went back into his tent.

Slowly, soddenly, he sank upon the rubber cover of his bunk looking fixedly and unseeingly at his fouled boots. *Da juju.* The devil, Ambu had called him. Had not Ambu been right? For what animal could do these things and remain out of the range of a hunter's guns? *Da juju—*

There was a slithering, harsh sound and Ginger, blenched white, came shaking to his feet, his light gun swinging toward the movement, sweat starting from him. But there was no target. The thrown-back flap of his tent had slipped into place, moved by the wind.

He was nauseated and for seconds the feeling of claws digging into his back would not abate. He struggled with his pent sanity, sought nervously for the key of control which, more and more, was ever beyond the reach of mental fingers. The scream died unvoiced, the gun slipped to the bunk and lay there with its muzzle like a fixed, accusing eye. Hypnotically, Ginger Cranston looked at that muzzle. It threw a twenty-millimeter slug and would tear half a head from a Mamodon bull; the bullet came out when the trigger was pressed, came out with a roar of savage flame, came out with oblivion as its command. Limply Ginger regarded it. He knew very little about death, he a hunter who should have known so much. Was death a quiet and untroubled sleep which went on forever or was death a passing to another existence? Would the wings of death carry something that was really Ginger Cranston out of this compound, away from these trees, this fog, this constant rain, this . . . this beast?

Funny he had never before considered death, odd how little he knew, he who had been so sure and proud of knowing so very much.

Death was a final conclusion—or was it a beginning? And if he took it now— Suddenly he saw where his thought led him and drew back in terror from the lip of the chasm. Then, as one who wonders how far he would have fallen had he slipped, he crept cautiously back and thoughtfully regarded the bottomless, unknowable deep, finding within himself at this strange moment a power to regard such a thing with a detached attitude, to dispassionately weigh a thing which he believed it to be in his hand to choose.

He seemed to fall away from himself in body and yet stand there, an untouchable, uncaring personality who had but to extend a crooking finger and call unto himself all there was to know. Suspended in time, in action, in human thought, he regarded all he was, had been, would be. There were no words to express this identity, this timelessness, only a feeling of actually existing for the first time; layer upon layer of a nameless something had been peeled away to leave a naked, knowing thing; a mask was gone from his eyes. But when he again came to himself, still standing beside his bed, still staring at the gun, he was muddy, weary Ginger Cranston once again who could feel that something had happened but could not express even in nebulous thought any part of the occurrence. Something had changed. A decision had been born. A plan of action, a somber, solemn plan was his.

About his waist he buckled a flame pistol and into that belt he thrust a short skinning knife. He pulled up his collar and strapped his swamp mask to it. He picked up his gun and looked into its magazine.

When Ginger stepped from the tent the chief was gone but the bottle sat upright in the mud, untouched, a reproof which would have reached Ginger a few minutes before but which could not touch him now. For perhaps an hour, even a day, nothing could touch him, neither sadness nor triumph. He was still within himself, waiting for a thing he knew would come, a thing much greater than shame or sorrow. He had chosen his death, for he had found it to be within his realm of choice and having chosen it he was dead. It mattered little what happened now. It mattered much that *da juju* would end. But it did not matter emotionally. It was a clear concern, undiluted by self.

Walking quietly through the mud he came to the trail which led upward to the series of knolls where the trees were thinner and the ground a degree more solid. This time he was not tracking. He gave no heed to the ground, for he was within the role of the hunted, not that of the hunter. He knew with a clarity not born of reason that he would be found.

Along the crest of a small hill, looking out across the foggy depths of the forest, touched faintly by the gloomy sun, he walked and knew he could be seen against the sky. He stopped a little while and dispassionately regarded the forest tops again, noting for the first time that gray was not the color there as he had always supposed but drab green, rust red, dark blue and smoky yellow. It was a little thing to notice but it seemed important. He turned and walked slowly back along the crest, gun held in the crook of his arm, his body relaxed. From this end he could see the impression of the village, a vacant space in the trees, a small knoll itself, wrapped in blue yellow cotton batting which restively shifted pattern.

About him the clouds thickened blindingly and the lenses of his swamp mask fogged. For a brief instant terror was in him before he pressed it gently down, out of sight, and buried it somewhere within him once more. The clouds lifted and curved easily away. For a little while then the sun was almost bright and it was this time upon which he had counted. He could be seen for a kilometer or more against the sky, blackly etched, motionless, waiting.

The atmosphere thickened, darkened, grew soggier with spurts of rain; the sun and any trace of it vanished even to Ginger's shadow. The time was here. He would walk slowly, leaving deep tracks, putting aside any impulse to step on stone and so break his trail. He knew *it* would follow.

He took his time, now and then pausing to arrange some imagined opening in his coat or his mask, occasionally pulling off the mask altogether and lighting his pipe, to sit on a rotten log until the tobacco was wholly burned.

He had no plan of walking save that he stayed in the trees where the great branches leaned out above him like grasping hands, only half seen in the gloom.

When the dark began to settle he did not return to the village, but kept upon his circuitous way, vaguely aware that the compound was somewhere upon his right, caring very little about it.

When he could no longer see clearly he groped to the base of a great tree; he could sit here now, waiting with dull patience for the thing to happen. From his pocket he took his pipe and pouch. From his face he pulled the swamp mask. Steadying his gun against the trunk beside him he proceeded to prepare his smoke.

It happened suddenly, silently, efficiently. The vine-woven net dropped soundlessly over his head, slithered to his feet and then with swift ferocity, yanked tight and brought him with a crash into the mud!

There was a scurrying about him as though something leaped up and down, darted back and forth to swiftly study the situation so as to require a minimum of effort in the final kill.

Ginger's right hand sought to grip the flame pistol at his thigh, but he could not bend his arm; his left hand clawed insensately at the net and a scream of terror welled up in his throat. He stilled the beating of the hand. He pressed back the scream. He reached to his belt and drew the knife with a deliberate swiftness and an economy of effort. The keen edge bit into the tough fibers of the vine, cleared it away from half his side, began to slice it off his ankles. And then the thing struck!

The vine-woven net dropped soundlessly over his head,
slithered to his feet and then with swift ferocity,
yanked tight and brought him with a crash into the mud!

The foul animal smell of it assailed him, more acute than the bite of the claws which went through his jacket and into his side like a set of bayonets.

He sensed the downward drive of the other claws and caught a blurred glimpse of the thing. The slimy fur of the leg was in his fingers and the striking paw missed his face.

Ginger jabbed upward with the knife and felt it saw vainly into the thing. With a scream the beast twisted away and with it went the knife.

There was a brief interval before the next, more savage attack, and in that space Ginger cleared his feet of the net. When it struck him again, like a battering ram with force enough to smash in his ribs, he was able to come to his knees and fumble for his flame pistol while fending with his left arm. He had no more than drawn the gun when a scrambling kick sent it flying into the mud, far from reach.

A cold piece of metal banged Ginger in the mouth and he snatched hungrily for the haft of his flesh-imbedded knife. Slippery as his fingers were, he retained it, drew it forth. He kicked out with his feet and then drove the keen steel deep into the body of the thing!

With a shudder it fell back, a claw weakly seeking to strike again and then falling away. There was a threshing, rattling sound and Ginger drew away, trying to clear his sight, fumbling with the other hand for his gun which he knew had been at the base of the tree. He had the weapon in his hand before he could see. There was water in a footprint which his hand had touched and he quickly bathed his eyes.

The light was faint, too faint to show more than a dark blob stretched in the muck, a blob which didn't move now. Ginger warily skirted it, keeping it covered, fumbling for a flash inside his waterproof coat.

The cold, impersonal beam played upon the object, raked it from end to end and then strayed uncertainly back to the head.

Ginger knelt and unfastened the straps of the frayed, worn, leatherlike suit that clothed the corpse and laboriously turned it over. Metal-tipped space gloves clicked as the arms flopped against each other. There was an almost illegible trace of lettering on the back, fouled with mud and blood, torn in spots. "SP——E SHII——" it said, before a gouge tore out the ship's name. Below, "Spacepo——Lowry, U——A."

It stank with dried and rotted blood and meat of long-gone kills, and the unwashed body of its occupant.

Ginger turned it back and looked again at the face. Identification was hopeless. The disastrous landing had gouged and torn the face half away; there was a deep dent in the forehead where the skull had been broken inward, and an angry, seamed and cross-seamed welt told of slow healing without the slightest rudiments of attention.

Ginger straightened slowly, gathered his things from the ground, and squelched off on his backtrail. Native bearers would have to carry that beast home. The beast some unknown and probably unknowable crash of a small tramp spacer had made from a man. A ruthless, pure animal—with all the cunning of human intelligence still left in the damaged brain.

Ginger swung along the trail in the long, easy strides of a huntsman of standing. There were bruises, and certain scratches that twinged a bit, but that sort of damage was of no importance. The great thing was—a thing Ginger now scarcely realized—that he had recaptured that quite intangible reality that had been stolen from him.

THE SLAVER

THE SLAVER

VORIS SHAPADIN heard the shot and lurched back in his chair in surprise, staring at the port and holding the leg of a chicken halfway between table and beard.

Somewhere in the *Gaffgon* footbeats pounded toward a gun. The insect-stained face of the intership communicator panel lit and the scarred visage of the navigator flickered there.

"Party returning to the ship, sir."

Voris yanked the napkin from his fat neck and snatched up the rusty helmet which he wore in preference to a peaked cap. The helmet had ray burns on it and the strap was rotted half through with sweat; it made Voris feel important because it was an officer's field helmet and he had never been higher than a feldcapal in the Outer War. When he stood up, bits of food rolled off his lap, bouncing from bulge to bulge and finally to the decayed spring carpet.

Voris took his belt gun and holster from the fever-flattened servant and went up the treacherously greasy ladder to the bridge.

Another shot racketed through the half-open dodger, and Voris prodded his way between his navigator and a quartermaster to a point of vantage in the wing.

"What the scatterbrained hell is that all about out there?" demanded Voris without turning to his navigator.

"I dunno, sir. Doesn't sound like our guns." The navigator ventured this with timidity, although he was not timid in appearance. He had on a sweater striped horizontally and striped again with liquor stains, and over this he wore a jacket of battered green and threadbare lace; there were two ray scorches on the jacket. The navigator's face was misshapen on one side where flame had left a ghastly splotch and had put out his eye. He wore no patch nor glass orb and left the socket dark and empty. He eyed his captain's back with respect prompted by an evil man's recognition of an even blacker personality.

Noisily, Voris sucked the shreds of chicken out of his spraddled teeth and spat the fragments over the side of the dodger. He wiped his mouth with a grease-slicked cuff and ranged his tiny white eyes over the scenery in growing impatience.

The *Gaffgon* was landed in a field of half-matured corn now cooked by the retarding blasts which had eased the old hulk down. She was a dreary pile of corrosion, the *Gaffgon*, for her propulsion was accomplished with the old vent principle, and the small jets which made her look like a scaled monster had also made her filthy with farillium soot. She presented a bad comparison with the cleanliness of this rural countryside.

A thick fringe of elms stood about this hilltop cornfield and barred much of the rolling country from view. The top of a steeple showed white and clean out of the valley, and a white road curved over the checkerboard horizon.

Voris Shapadin disliked this world intensely for its flatness, for he had been raised amid craggy peaks and ice rivers on Lurga, and the monotony of the present scenery combined with its heat to scratch his nerves.

He could hear men threshing about behind the screen of trees and knew from their far-off shouts that something was going wrong. It was very unusual to find any resistance in this place, and that alone had been its appeal, for one got his belly full of fighting in the outer lanes of Lurga, and men who could be trusted were too scarce to be risked in stupid skirmishes with stupid natives.

There was a sudden movement of shrubs and a small being burst out into the corn and ran several exhausted steps before he saw that he was heading for the *Gaffgon*. The footing was treacherous, and when he sought to halt in midrace he fell, flinging a black object away from him.

"Hold!" yelled a guard at the gangway. "Hold, there!"

The small being flipped to his feet and scooped up the black object. Voris could not make out the identity of the thing, but he felt it was a weapon of some sort.

A squad was running out through the corn from the *Gaffgon*, and sailors had broken from the trees to spread out and converge upon their quarry. The small being was trapped, but his attitude was one of frenzied defiance. He was doing something to the black object.

The two groups made a circle around him some thirty yards wide. The small being stood still for a moment and pointed at a sailor with the black object. There was a stab of thunder, and the sailor was thrown back in a jackknife.

"Shoot him!" howled Voris from his bridge. "Shoot the pig!"

A sailor had the small being from behind, but there was a blur of action and another crash of thunder, and the sailor, already dead, was dropped to earth. The small being tried madly to get away from the others. No one could fire at him, so thick was the press. And then, by crushing him to earth and beating at his head with gun butts, the sailors at last had him.

"The fools!" said Voris. "Two men dead! Maybe more! Is that worth the price of one man? He'll bring less than twenty weights in the market, and two sailors— Vash! Wait until we get him aboard and in irons!"

Voris hastened down the ladder to the gangway to await the arrival of the group.

From another part of the fringe of trees a line of people was emerging, silent save for the clank of chains. To these, the bulk of his cargo, Voris gave no heed, for the sight was common enough to him.

The sailors, carrying their single captive, leaving their dead where they had fallen, reached the bottom of the gangway. Their faces were scarlet with exertion and their ragged white uniforms sodden with sweat. The bos'n in the lead halted when he saw Voris, and realized for the first time that the group was liable to punishment for having conducted the matter so badly. The bos'n squared his thick shoulders and put a blank expression upon his bearded face. He continued on up the gangway and gave Voris a doubtful salute.

Voris said nothing. He waited until the others had come

into the ship and had thrown amid the refuse of the deck their hard-won game.

The captive was young, and though he was bloodied by the gun butts, he was seen to be of regular features. His body was slender, which was not a good sign, for he would not be able to stand up under a great deal of hard labor. He was blond. He was an aristocrat. He was, Voris decided instantly, no good whatever.

Voris started to speak, and then found that he had no words equal to this. He ranged his white eyes from face to face and cursed them all with a silence which was far more horrible than verbal blasts.

With a jerk of his head, dismissing the men into the ship, Voris swept them with the blackness of his contempt. Then he kicked the captive in the side with a heavy space boot, and when the man did not stir, kicked him in the face. The captive lay as one dead.

The silent column was now coming up the gangway, and Voris, with a final kick, stepped back to survey them.

There were about a hundred and fifty people in the line. About a quarter of them were women. These last had been selected for form and face, and though they were tear-stained and bedraggled now, they would bring a good enough price on Lurga. The rest were men in their twenties and thirties, most of them sullen, some of them beaten, none of them defiant. They were laborers and mechanics possessing toil-hardened hands and wind-darkened faces, selected because of strength or possible deftness with material.

One by one the chained captives stepped over the young man on the deck. A face here and there lighted for an instant in startled recognition, and then instantly went blank, as though afraid to be found knowing this one who had obviously put up a battle.

Only one face in all that line contained any fire. Her eyes were an astonishing shade of blue, and her face and body contained strength as well as beauty. Her cheek was bruised where she had been struck, and the cotton garment was ripped away from her shoulder so that she had to hold it in place. When she saw Voris her ripe mouth curved down on one side and her attitude hardened into contempt. She was on the point of spitting at the commander when the presence of the young man on the floor caught her attention. She paused, startled, only to be yanked forward by the chain which connected her to the next captive. She was very careful not to step on the man, and then shot Voris a glare which was of withering violence.

Voris was suddenly cheerful. He momentarily forgot his loss of men. He looked after the woman and laughed quietly.

So amused was Voris Shapadin that he showed only slight annoyance to the spotting agent who came a few minutes later to collect his reward.

Deep in the reeking hold of the *Gaffgon*, where darkness and misery and stench caught in the throat to strangle, Kree Lorin of Falcon's Nest came slowly to his senses and struggled to rise. But chains clanked to jeer his effort and pulled him down again. Stupidly he felt for his knife, then fumbled on the floor about him for his gun. The loss of the two served to speed returning sensibility.

One by one the chained captives stepped over the young man on the deck. A face here and there lighted for an instant in startled recognition, and then instantly went blank, as though afraid to be found knowing this one who had obviously put up a battle.

He stared through the dimness and caught a hazy impression of the hold, of two tiers of captives, people felt rather than seen, for the only light came from three blue bulbs studding the upper bulkhead.

Here were at least three hundred human beings reduced to the last depths of degradation and despair, reduced even below the point of whimpering, as though they recognized already the finality of their fate, as though they knew that only two-thirds of them would reach Lurga alive and that half of those who remained would sweat out their lives in the factories and on the fields of that planet in the first two years of their captivity.

Kree Lorin's head felt as though a grenade had burst in it. He was a dull stupidity floating above the red blur of pain which was his body. Searchingly he sought to piece together the why of his presence, but the facts were too final and damning to be reached. He could not believe that he was here.

In a little while he would get up and go home. He would dismount before the big gray gates of the stronghold and pass his reins into the hands of a groom and, grasping the partridges he had shot, would saunter across the court and into the big dining hall, where his father would meet him with a proud and stern face which yet could not hide gleaming fondness.

His homecoming would be a little unusual this time, for he would be twenty-one on the morrow, and there was preparation for a celebration to welcome him into manhood.

A lackey would strip off his spurs, would take the birds

and gun. Another would appear with a tray of wine and sweetbread. And then he would relate to his father the chances of the hunt—

A captive screamed in the fetid gloom. Kree Lorin raised his head and stared, and all the dismal weight of this obscene place crushed its way into his heart. Suddenly he wanted to scream an answer back. He wanted to call the guards and batter them with his chains. He could not be here. He, Kree Lorin of Falcon's Nest, could never be a slave!

So this was what it meant. To be robbed of hope forever. To be chained and herded against humanity in the airless dark of a spaceship hull. To be carried to some terrifying far place and there be sold among enemies!

He, Kree Lorin, was a soldier! His father had fought in those last devastating wars. He himself had been trained to the rifle and grenade. And in anticipation of yet other battles and revolts, he had been made to study the tongue of the Lurga Empire, the structure of spaceships, the rudiments of that vast complexity which was military and mechanical science in the year of Defeat Thirty-nine.

Once Earth had had its fleets to scourge the blackness of outer space. Once Earth had been a proud mistress of great empire, not a vassal planet led willfully into decay by the conquerors. He, Kree Lorin, had been brought up a soldier against the day of revolt—

The sultry gloom gagged him and he moaned. There was a stir at his left and he choked off the sound, for it was deeply bred into him never to show weakness.

"You are Kree Lorin," said a dim blur which was a face beside him. There was a jarring note of amusement in the tone.

Kree looked fixedly at the white blur, and gradually traced its features. He felt no recognition clearly, but only that he should know this girl.

"Kree Lorin," she said, "in the hold of a slaver!" It was nearly laughter.

He hitched himself up on his elbow and stared at her, and gradually the mists in his mind cleared away. He knew her now. The peasant girl of Palmerton. The peasant girl he had seized off the dusty road, lifting her saddle-high to attempt a kiss upon her lovely mouth. His own cheek stung for an instant in memory.

Yes, this was she, Dana of Palmerton, whom he had afterward tried to bring to Falcon's Nest by bribing her slut of a mother. Dana of Palmerton, who would rather live in a corncrib a free woman than a pampered slavey in mighty Falcon's Nest!

"They got you, too?" he muttered, feeling that it was a stupid remark.

"Me. I was made for a slave. But Kree Lorin, the young hawk of Falcon's Nest—" She laughed.

He wanted to strike her, but the thought of the effort robbed him of what strength he had, and he sank down to the slippery filth of the metal deck.

Evidently she was but lightly chained, for she moved to his side. With rough but efficient hands she turned him over and untangled his irons. She tore a strip from her dress and dampened it in her water cup to bathe away the blood and grime which lay so thickly on him.

She worked silently, taking other strips from her clothing for bandages. There was a detached disdain in her which roughened his nerves; but the coolness she brought his hurts made him bear her attitude in silence.

When she had finished she did not move away, but remained there, looking at him, and he turned his face from her to become even more conscious of her regard.

There was a shock in the ship, and Kree felt his weight double, then treble. There was a vibrating roar which grew in volume and crescendo, and then faded slowly. His weight did not lessen, and for the first time he knew the sensation of flight. He felt a little afraid, and turned back to find that Dana's eyes were still on him. He wanted to give her some sharp rebuke, but somehow everything had changed.

He, Kree Lorin of Falcon's Nest, had been accustomed to obedience from the people of the province. Just how or why he had never bothered to reason. He had not questioned his right until now that he was robbed of it. She, Dana of Palmerton, had a better command of the situation than he. She was therefore higher, somehow, than he. She, suddenly, was the superior being.

Puzzled, he looked at her for a long while. And then, because the increased weight made him ache anew, he began to slowly lose his hold on clarity and relapse back into a fog of half-felt pain.

He muttered without belief, "I am Kree Lorin. Kree Lorin of Falcon's Nest." But the name sounded very far away and meaningless.

Hours blended and blurred and stretched themselves into

a dismal chain of aching monotony wherein commingled the stench of the ship, the whimpering of the cargo, and all the gloomy suffering of silent men who knew that so many others had gone this way, never to return, and that the end of the voyage would only begin a more degrading phase.

Air was too precious to be changed. Water was too scarce to be wasted. And capsule food, a thing to which these people were not used, accelerated their enfeeblement. Such stress pressed down their perceptions, and they might have been a week in space or a year for all they could recall. At first they had sometimes talked, sometimes there had been an attempt at song. But now no talk and certainly no song could be found in them.

Voris Shapadin walked through this cargo hold once, a scented rag held up to his nostrils, and berated the guard for not perceiving that at least eight here were dying, would die before the voyage was over, and so should not be permitted to exhaust stores.

After Voris Shapadin had gone, four guards in masks came and removed the victims, striking one who was so tenacious of life even in the face of slavery that he complained wildly and even sought to fight as he was borne away.

Kree Lorin lay still and watched with half-lidded eyes. He was too deadened by suffering to be much affected. He found himself faintly wishing that that had been meted to him. And so he was slightly amazed that the girl Dana should throw a pannikin at one of the guards who dragged at the protesting one.

She had paid little attention to Kree Lorin, as though she found him too despicable for notice. Dimly he understood that there is no state lower than that of one who has fallen from a height.

From Falcon's Nest the Lorins had foraged out to extract a sort of tax or tribute from the peasantry on the slight excuse that the presence of an armed body prevented an incursion by the people beyond the river. A rough sort of court was occasionally held whereat peasants could find justice of a sort. But though out of fear the Lorins were respected, no soldier was liked. "Soldier" was a word of contempt, had become so within the memory of these people when the legions and fleets of Earth had been battered into rubble. And now from Falcon's Nest had come forth a son as a slave, despised and bludgeoned and defeated by his captors, and even lower now, had dropped any prestige Kree Lorin might have had.

Kree Lorin knew this. He knew a great many things out of books, out of the forest paths. He knew how easily men died. He himself had seen men die through the sights of his rifle. But for the first time he knew how easily he himself could die. Unlike these peasants he had known no filth, little suffering beyond the rigors of the chase. And he felt that that which was he had been defiled and smashed. Had he had the slightest hope he would also have found defiance. But he had no hope and he was ill. And it was no wonder, he thought vaguely, that she despised him.

They were gone, the guards and the eight who had been condemned. Voris Shapadin came back and flashed a light down the rows of prisoners while his sailors executed a swift search. A knife had been found upon a dying man and two knives were brought from concealment by this second inspection.

Voris Shapadin did not flatter Kree Lorin with any particular attention. In fact, he seemed to have forgotten that anything unusual had happened in the capture of this man. The sailors stirred Kree Lorin up and made a perfunctory examination of his ragged clothing, and the light in the commander's hand passed on to fix Dana in a dull yellow glow.

The sailors grinned as they started to search her and she struck viciously, and the crack of her hand on the leathery jaw made Voris Shapadin chuckle.

"Leave her," he said. And the sailors passed to the next.

Kree Lorin lay where he was and thought fitfully about Dana. The light had shown her to him again after this endless period of darkness, and the startling blue of her angry eyes had recalled him to the fact that he had spent many weeks thinking about her back on Earth, and that he had tried very hard to somehow win her.

What might have been an hour, what might have been a day later, he awoke from a troubled dream and looked around him in the gloom. The odor of filth and death, the whimper of a captive, bit into him sharply.

It was a startling thing to him, a thing which was incredible and defied explanation.

He raised himself on his elbow and looked down the long tunnel of the cargo hold and the three blue bulbs, and felt the peculiarly weightless sensation of flight.

Suddenly it seemed to Kree Lorin that a nightmare had turned real, for he had absolutely no explanation of his whereabouts, no memory of having arrived there, no idea of where he was going. He felt of the bandages which had swathed his head and pulled them off, wondering how he had been hurt.

The sensations which stirred in him lasted for perhaps a minute, and then, as one looks through a shadowy window, he recalled what had occurred. But why was all that so dull and all this so sharp?

Had he gone through an illness? Was he just now recovering from a fever of wounds?

What was different about his state today?

And then he knew. And knew why things were so sharp. And knew with an awful dread. For the chains of the bulkhead next to him were hanging empty.

He looked at the man on his right and prodded him. "What has happened to the woman who was chained here?"

Disinterestedly the slave grunted, "They came for her a while ago."

"When?"

"A while ago. What does it matter?" He buried his head in the crook of his arm and muttered, "What does anything matter?"

Kree Lorin thought of the sailors who had searched her, of the grin of the commander. And then instantly stopped his thoughts.

He rattled his chains and yanked at them, and for a moment felt something give. But the hope was false, for a kink had turned straight, and there was no freeing the great rings in the bulkhead. He rattled his chains, and the noise added to his anger. He banged them loudly against the plates and then began to double the noise and yell.

Here and there a slave took it up. The din grew. Kree Lorin raved and the slaves bellowed and screamed, glad to break the silence of this place.

The din continued for several minutes before any result was achieved, and then the door at the end of the hold opened and a guard came in, a pool of light about his feet, his gun ready in hand.

"Stop!" cried the guard in Lurgese.

"Come and stop me!" roared Kree, for though his knowledge might not be perfect, he had been taught against some day of victory the tongue of the conqueror.

The guard called for support and then advanced down the center of the hold toward Kree. Two other guards followed him into the place.

"Your mothers were swine!" cried Kree. "Your children are dogs!"

The guard in the lead played his light upon the frenzied slave and noted the unnatural brilliance of eye and the grayness of the cheeks.

"Stop this noise!"

"Make me!" bellowed Kree. "I have the spacard! I know that I have it, and if I choose to die now instead of tomorrow—Shoot! You don't dare shoot! Your brothers are goats and you dine on filth! Shoot me!"

The guard faltered and looked uneasily at his companions.

For it was very weird to hear an Earthman screaming Lurgese. And it was nothing for jest—spacard—the thing which had swept more than one ship into aimless orbits in space.

The trio became conscious of their hand weapons, and Kree, watching, knew that he was close to being shot. But instead, one of the guards drew away and came back shortly with a small Lurgan in a gold cap which bore the insignia of medicine.

The small doctor was holding a kerchief to his nose. His footing was uncertain, and he appeared to be drunk.

"Spacard, is it?" he said, his voice muffled in the kerchief. "Bring him outside and we'll know soon enough. Bah, what a pesthole!"

Kree, who had only wanted the guards within range of his swinging chain, had not hoped for this much. He subsided while a sailor put on a mask and approached him to unlock his irons from the ringbolts.

Making him walk at a safe distance before them and under their guns, they took him out into the passage and slammed the hold door. Even though the passage lights were not exceptionally bright, they were like dirks into Kree's eyes.

Prodded ahead and bumping into the bulkheads, so unsteady had he become during the passage, Kree was forced into a small room which reeked of antiseptics and alcohol. He caught a glimpse of himself in an instrument cabinet door and was repelled by his own appearance. Haggard and unshaven, filthy and ragged, he little resembled the Kree Lorin who had gone forth to the hunt such an infinite time ago.

The doctor reeled into a chair and looked fixedly at the captive. "Spacard, is it?" he hiccuped. "Lie down on that table."

Chains clanking, Kree stretched himself out on the cold metal. He knew that the sole reason for all this attention proceeded from the necessity of inoculating slaves and crew if it was proved that he did have spacard. A more vigilant doctor might have done the inoculation at the beginning of the voyage just for safety, but this was the *Gaffgon*, a derelict and slaver, not a transport or war vessel.

The sailors were afraid to approach Kree, but under the medico's insistence began to buckle his ankles down.

To them, Kree had appeared wild without purpose and weaving from weakness. They only feared the germs which he might carry. They did not envision the danger of those confining chains which looped down from his wrists. Not until there was a rattle and swish and the dull crunch of inburst bone. A sailor went down.

A gun came up and the wielder's face turned into a red spatter. The medico squealed and then fell, his hands plucking at his head in lessening strength. The third sailor would have run had he been between Kree and the door. He was not. His gun was smashed from his hand. The horror of the slave's appearance and the death which had struck the others numbed the remaining man's mind. He thought about his gun, but not soon enough. The chain caught him against the bulkhead, and for two or three seconds he stood there.

Kree was panting, but sustained by a fire of victory which physical exertion could not quench. There was raw hate in him, and he did not let the man who began to struggle on the floor come farther than one elbow before he crushed him down again.

They were dead, all of them. The white walls of the examination room were brightened. Kree took their keys and freed his wrists of the iron. He took their guns and girded them about his waist.

He entertained no great hopes, for such a ship would be forever on guard, but he made no incautious moves, for there was bred into him with the soldier the caution of the hunter. From the flagon on the wall he took a long drink, and the water was like life flowing through him. From the surgeon's cabinet he took a hidden store of condensed food. From a less marked sailor he took a jacket and a cap he picked up from under the table. He added a razor and soap to his loot and then stepped to the door.

The companionway was clear. He fumbled with the latch as he closed it, but his hands shook a little and he had no patience with the combination. Afraid that he would be found there if he stayed longer, he had to abandon his effort to lock the door, no matter the danger of premature discovery to which the contents of that room might lead.

The long passageway was naked and without side corridors. He came to its end and saw a ladder leading up. At the top of it stood a sailor, facing the other way and leaning against the supporting chains which held the hatch open.

Kree went up, cat-footed. The butt of a pistol fell once and then twice. He tried to haul the body out of sight behind the hatch, but it was too large and one boot protruded. He did not dare linger there, and again was forced to leave a mark of his way behind.

This was a boat deck, and the spaceboats were in the bulges which jutted into the ship to preserve its streamline. Kree had had no practice with anything like these, and he had groaned, as a boy, over the insistence of old Colonel Stauckner that such things should be known. He had yawned then. Now he apprehensively studied the air lock and tried to recall the theory. Perhaps if he opened that thing while not in a spacesuit he would be ballooned into a thing of horror. He peered through the cloudy pane and saw the hooded spaceboat's interior. This was a thing he had to chance now, not afterward. He opened the lock. There was a swirl of air around him which eddied into quietness. The stale interior of the *Gaffgon* made the musty air of the spaceboat a welcome thing. He entered and shut the lock and scanned the gloom around him.

He was thankful that the *Gaffgon* was nearly as old as the texts from which Colonel Stauckner had attempted to give him a broad education. But even more than the texts, his own sense of logic helped him. In Lurgese most of the panel was named. To launch, it was evident that one closed the spaceboat's lock, reached through and threw the catch on the confining door and then blasted the small vessel against the door and out into space. It seemed simple enough. He hoped that he could do it. He was afraid he would not remember the outer catch and threw it now with some qualms. Nothing happened. He felt better.

Now that he knew where he was going and what he would do, he turned back to the lock, opened it and peered up and down the *Gaffgon*'s upper passage. It was empty.

Dodging from bulge to bulge, he made his way forward. He nearly blundered into a sleeping compartment and then into another slave hold before he located the ladder which must lead up to the bridge.

Momentarily expecting to be stopped, he went up. Just as his eyes came on a level with the upper deck a gong began to clang, answered in deafening alarm by other gongs throughout the ship. Some one of his traces had been discovered!

He scrambled into a niche behind the hatch cover and crouched there, trying to decide which door before him was Voris Shapadin's, and in that moment his answer came to him. The commander dashed from his cabin, buckling a gun about his waist. From the dimness, Kree saw that Shapadin's mouth was torn and bleeding, and that his shirt collar had been ripped. There was frustrated anger in the man which drove him now to seek revenge upon whomever should fall in his pathway.

He whirled as he started down and cried to the officer of the watch, visible through the bridge door, "Post a guard over that hellcat! Which hold is it?"

"No. 3, sir," said the officer. "A sailor found the medico dead with the No. 3 guards!"

"Send men to me down there!" roared Shapadin and leaped out of sight.

The bridge officer was turning to his tubes. Kree flitted by the door and came to Shapadin's quarters.

Dana's composure, up to this moment, had remained under control. She stood now against the table, defiance in her bearing and flame in her eyes, holding her dress together with a clenched fist. There was a bruise on her cheek, but there was proud victory upon her mouth.

And then she saw Kree and recognized him. Her body started and her face flooded with incredulity. And then a mist swam before her eyes and she stumbled toward him.

Kree glanced back down the ladder into the noisy ship. A guard was coming up to take over his appointed duty. Kree stepped deeper into the room and gripped Dana's hand. He unlimbered a gun and held it loosely.

The sailor stepped through the door, and Kree shot him between the eyes.

"Come on!" said Kree, and hurried Dana beside him.

The officer on watch turned toward the door, not much alarmed, for shot and footfalls were swallowed in the dinning gongs. Kree fired from the waist, and then in the few seconds he thought he could spare, began to smash the fire control panel and throttles with a series of flame cartridges.

"Look out!" screamed Dana into the clamor.

Kree ducked and then spun. The shot went over his head. His own aim was not as bad, for the guard went tumbling backward down the ladder, to lie inertly at the bottom.

In the confusion, Kree tried to recall the way he had come, but almost immediately took a wrong corridor. They came out on the boat deck, but it was port, not starboard, where he was sure of his spaceboat and its equipment.

Somewhere Shapadin was beginning a sweep of the whole vessel, and Kree knew he stood little chance unless he also had the advantage of surprise.

Kree dragged the girl through a door and they found themselves in an officer's pantry. An attendant cowered away from them and vanished through another door before Kree could stop him.

Abruptly the gongs ceased. In the passage outside, the warning howl of the attendant went into the distance.

Kree stumbled across the wardroom with its threadbare cloth and scarred furniture and racked riot guns. He saw that two weapons had been left in the rack and took one of them. But with this type of weapon he had no experience and could not quickly load it. He cast it away from him and drew his remaining belt gun. There were ten shots in this, all that remained to him.

The next two doors let them out on the boat deck on the starboard side, and Kree marked the spaceboat he had checked. It was a considerable distance up the deck from them, its door invitingly open.

They started toward it, and then there was a cry of discovery from behind them. Kree hurled the girl into a niche between the bulges and flattened himself against the side. A shot scored rust above his head, and another twitched at his belt.

He took careful aim, not allowing himself to be disturbed. A man in the group two hundred feet up the deck screamed and spun about. The others hurriedly dodged back into cover, while Voris Shapadin, behind them, bullied them.

Kree indicated that the girl should run for the open door, and he himself began to back toward it, firing carefully at each face which presented itself at the turn of the passage.

The range was extreme for a flame gun of the belt type. And as his shots missed, the sailors began to gather courage.

Step by step he worked his way back. Cartridge by cartridge he neared the open door where Dana had already arrived. He counted seven. He counted eight.

He whirled and raced for it. A chunk of metal flew out of the door before his outstretched hand. Dana snatched at him and helped him through.

Kree turned in this cover and fired his ninth shot. The group was racing toward him now and the men were hard to hit. Kree took very careful aim. He squeezed the trigger, keeping his arm properly loose. The gun recoiled.

Voris Shapadin curled up into an agonized knot on the deck, his speed causing him to tumble three yards farther.

Kree slammed the port. He smashed the heel of his hand against the jet buttons.

There was a crash as the outer port went up. Speed jammed the two against the seats and momentarily blinded them.

After a little he cut the acceleration and eased down into position so that he could discover the use of the controls and the answerability of the jet helm.

He looked across the black skies and all around, but he found no sign of the *Gaffgon*. He looked critically at various stars which blazed through the airless void. One, quite near, was gigantic. And near it there was a planet.

Kree became aware of the girl beside him. Her wonderously blue eyes were fixed upon him as though she were hypnotized.

And then, as though she herself had only begun to believe it, she said, "You . . . I . . . escaped!"

He was getting his equilibrium back now. He grinned at her. She dropped her glance in humility and leaned a little closer to him.

"I . . . I'm sorry for what—"

"Sorry?" said Kree. "Sorry for what?"

"But you . . . are a . . . a very brave and—" She looked at him mistily.

"Brave? Why," said Kree with an offhand wave of his arm, "why, of course I'm brave. I am Kree Lorin. Kree Lorin of Falcon's Nest."

STORY PREVIEW

STORY PREVIEW

NOW that you've just ventured through some of the captivating tales in the Stories from the Golden Age collection by L. Ron Hubbard, turn the page and enjoy a preview of *The Professor Was a Thief*. Join Pop, a down-on-his-luck reporter needing a big story—one he finds after the Empire State Building, Grant's Tomb and Grand Central Station disappear. When Pop digs deeper, he discovers a professor behind it all who, rather than inventing a means of blowing things up, is doing quite the opposite.

THE PROFESSOR WAS A THIEF

NO one knew why he was called Pop unless it was that he had sired the newspaper business. For the first few hundred years, it appeared, he had been a senior reporter, going calmly about his business of reporting wholesale disaster, but during the past month something truly devastating had occurred. Muttering noises sounded in the ranks.

Long overdue for the job of city editor, lately vacated via the undertaker, Pop had been demoted instead of promoted. Ordinarily Pop was not a bitter man. He had seen too many cataclysms fade into the staleness of yesterday's paper. He had obit-ed too large a legion of generals, saints and coal heavers to expect anything from life but its eventual absence. But there were limits.

When Leonard Caulborn, whose diapers Pop had changed, had been elevated to city editor over Pop's decaying head, Pop chose to attempt the dissolution of Gaul in the manufactures of Kentucky. But even the latter has a habit of wearing away and leaving the former friend a mortal enemy. Thus it was, when the copy boy came for him, that Pop swore at the distilleries as he arose and looked about on the floor where he supposed his head must have rolled.

"Mr. Caulborn said he hada seeyuh rightaway," said the copy boy.

Pop limped toward the office, filled with resentment.

Leonard Caulborn was a wise young man. Even though he had no real knowledge of the newspaper business, people *still* insisted he was wise. Hadn't he married the publisher's daughter? And if the paper didn't make as much as it should, didn't the publisher have plenty of stockholders who could take the losses and never feel them—much, anyway.

Young and self-made and officious if not efficient, Caulborn greeted Pop not at all, but let him stand before the desk a few minutes.

Pop finally picked up a basket and dropped it a couple inches, making Caulborn look up.

"You sent for me?" said Pop.

"I sent for you— Oh, yes, I remember now. Pending your retirement you've been put on the copy desk."

"My *what?*" cried Pop.

"Your retirement. We are retiring all employees over fifty. We need new people and new ideas here."

"Retirement?" Pop was still gaping. "When? How?"

"Effective day after tomorrow, Pop, you are no longer with this paper. Our present Social Security policy—"

"Will pay me off about twenty bucks complete," said Pop. "But to hell with that. I brought this paper into the world and it's going to take me out. You can't do this to me!"

"I have orders—"

"You are issuing the orders these days," said Pop. "What are you going to do for copy when you lose all your men that know the ropes?"

"We'll get along," said Caulborn. "That will be all."

"No, it won't either," said Pop. "I'm staying as reporter."

"All right. You're staying as reporter then. It's only two days."

"And you're going to give me assignments," said Pop.

Caulborn smiled wearily, evidently thinking it best to cajole the old coot. "All right, here's an article I clipped a couple months ago. Get a story on it."

When Caulborn had fished up the magazine out of his rubble-covered desk he tossed it to Pop like a citizen paying a panhandler.

Pop wanted to throw it back, for he saw at a glance that it was merely a stick, a rehash of some speech made a long while ago to some physics society. But he had gained ground so far. He wouldn't lose it. He backed out.

Muttering to himself he crossed to his own desk, wading through the rush and clamor of the city room. It was plain to him that he had to make the most of what he had. It was unlikely that he'd get another chance.

"I'll show 'em," he growled. "Call me a has-been. Well! Think I can't make a story out of nothing, does he? Why, I'll get such a story that he'll *have* to keep me on. And promote me. And raise my pay. Throw me into the gutter, will they?"

He sat down in his chair and scanned the article. It began quite lucidly with the statement that Hannibal Pertwee had made this address before the assembled physicists of the country. Pop, growing cold the while, tried to wade through said address. When he came out at the end with a spinning head he saw that Hannibal Pertwee's theories were not supported by anybody but Hannibal Pertwee. All other information, even to Pop, was so much polysyllabic nonsense. Something about transportation of freight. He gathered that much. Some new way to help civilization. But just how, the article did not tell—Pop, at least.

Suddenly Pop felt very old and very tired. At fifty-three he had ten thousand bylines behind him. He had built the *World-Journal* to its present importance. He loved the paper and now it was going to hell in the hands of an incompetent, and they were letting him off at a station halfway between nowhere and anywhere. And the only way he had of stopping them was an impossible article by some crackbrain on the transportation of freight.

He sighed and, between two shaking hands, nursed an aching head.

To find out more about *The Professor Was a Thief* and how you can obtain your copy, go to www.goldenagestories.com.

GLOSSARY

Stories from the Golden Age reflect the words and expressions used in the 1930s and 1940s, adding unique flavor and authenticity to the tales. While a character's speech may often reflect regional origins, it also can convey attitudes common in the day. So that readers can better grasp such cultural and historical terms, uncommon words or expressions of the era, the following glossary has been provided.

---

avarice: extreme greed for wealth or material gain.

batteries: groups of large-caliber weapons used for combined action.

beaters: people who drive animals out from cover.

beck: a gesture of the hand, head, etc., meant to summon.

bos'n: bosun; a petty officer on a merchant ship who supervises the work of the other crew.

brutes: animals other than human beings.

city room: the room in which local news is handled for a newspaper, a radio station or for another journalistic agency.

CPO: Chief Petty Officer.

crackbrain: a foolish, senseless or insane person.

dissolution of Gaul: "Pop chose to attempt the dissolution of Gaul in the manufactures of Kentucky" is a play on words, meaning that he tried to drown his bitter feelings in whiskey. The two words are *Gaul* and *gall*. *Gaul* was a territory in western Europe, which was dissolved (brought to an end) militarily by Julius Caesar in the first century BC and eventually became a Roman province. *Gall* is something bitter or distasteful; bitter feeling. The "manufactures of Kentucky" refers to whiskey produced in Kentucky.

dodger: a screen to provide protection on a ship.

dry washes: dry stream beds, as at the bottom of a canyon.

flagon: a container for beverages, with a handle, narrow neck, spout and sometimes a lid.

gangway: a narrow, movable platform or ramp forming a bridge by which to board or leave a ship.

G-men: government men; agents of the Federal Bureau of Investigation.

haft: the handle of a knife, axe or spear.

hard by: in close proximity to; near.

hither and thither: in many directions in a disorderly way.

juju: something thought to possess magical powers.

manufactures of Kentucky: whiskey made in Kentucky.

O: used in solemn or poetic language to add earnestness to an appeal.

obit-ed: a coined word meaning to write an obituary (a notice of a person's death, often with a short biography, in a newspaper).

obtained: existed.

pannikin: a small metal drinking cup.

Scheherazade: the female narrator of *The Arabian Nights,* who during one thousand and one adventurous nights saved her life by entertaining her husband, the king, with stories.

shoal: to become shallow.

slaver: a slave ship; a ship for transporting slaves from their native homes to places of bondage.

slug: a bullet.

spraddled: spread apart.

squelched: made a sucking sound (while walking on soft wet ground).

struck no colors: never surrendered. A variation of the phrase "striking the colors," which is the universally recognized sign of surrender for ships at battle; the flag is hauled down as a token of submission.

terrier who had no eyes for the size of her rats: *terrier* is a group of dogs initially bred for hunting and killing vermin, such as rats and small game, both above and under the ground. While usually small, these dogs are known for being brave and tough with a lively, energetic personality. They will tenaciously go after their prey, undeterred by its size, even digging into the ground if needed to reach it. Used figuratively.

thou: archaic form of *you.*

tramp: a freight vessel that does not run regularly between fixed ports, but takes a cargo wherever shippers desire.

vassals: servants or slaves.

Venusian: relating to the planet Venus.

L. Ron Hubbard
in the Golden Age
of Pulp Fiction

*In writing an adventure story
a writer has to know that he is adventuring
for a lot of people who cannot.
The writer has to take them here and there
about the globe and show them
excitement and love and realism.
As long as that writer is living the part of an
adventurer when he is hammering
the keys, he is succeeding with his story.*

*Adventuring is a state of mind.
If you adventure through life, you have a
good chance to be a success on paper.*

*Adventure doesn't mean globe-trotting,
exactly, and it doesn't mean great deeds.
Adventuring is like art.
You have to live it to make it real.*

— *L. RON HUBBARD*

L. Ron Hubbard
and American
Pulp Fiction

BORN March 13, 1911, L. Ron Hubbard lived a life at least as expansive as the stories with which he enthralled a hundred million readers through a fifty-year career.

Originally hailing from Tilden, Nebraska, he spent his formative years in a classically rugged Montana, replete with the cowpunchers, lawmen and desperadoes who would later people his Wild West adventures. And lest anyone imagine those adventures were drawn from vicarious experience, he was not only breaking broncs at a tender age, he was also among the few whites ever admitted into Blackfoot society as a bona fide blood brother. While if only to round out an otherwise rough and tumble youth, his mother was that rarity of her time—a thoroughly educated woman—who introduced her son to the classics of Occidental literature even before his seventh birthday.

But as any dedicated L. Ron Hubbard reader will attest, his world extended far beyond Montana. In point of fact, and as the son of a United States naval officer, by the age of eighteen he had traveled over a quarter of a million miles. Included therein were three Pacific crossings to a then still mysterious Asia, where he ran with the likes of Her British Majesty's agent-in-place

L. Ron Hubbard, left, at Congressional Airport, Washington, DC, 1931, with members of George Washington University flying club.

for North China, and the last in the line of Royal Magicians from the court of Kublai Khan. For the record, L. Ron Hubbard was also among the first Westerners to gain admittance to forbidden Tibetan monasteries below Manchuria, and his photographs of China's Great Wall long graced American geography texts.

Upon his return to the United States and a hasty completion of his interrupted high school education, the young Ron Hubbard entered George Washington University. There, as fans of his aerial adventures may have heard, he earned his wings as a pioneering barnstormer at the dawn of American aviation. He also earned a place in free-flight record books for the longest sustained flight above Chicago. Moreover, as a roving reporter for *Sportsman Pilot* (featuring his first professionally penned articles), he further helped inspire a generation of pilots who would take America to world airpower.

Immediately beyond his sophomore year, Ron embarked on the first of his famed ethnological expeditions, initially to then untrammeled Caribbean shores (descriptions of which would later fill a whole series of West Indies mystery-thrillers). That the Puerto Rican interior would also figure into the future of Ron Hubbard stories was likewise no accident. For in addition to cultural studies of the island, a 1932–33

LRH expedition is rightly remembered as conducting the first complete mineralogical survey of a Puerto Rico under United States jurisdiction.

There was many another adventure along this vein: As a lifetime member of the famed Explorers Club, L. Ron Hubbard charted North Pacific waters with the first shipboard radio direction finder, and so pioneered a long-range navigation system universally employed until the late twentieth century. While not to put too fine an edge on it, he also held a rare Master Mariner's license to pilot any vessel, of any tonnage in any ocean.

Yet lest we stray too far afield, there is an LRH note at this juncture in his saga, and it reads in part:

"I started out writing for the pulps, writing the best I knew, writing for every mag on the stands, slanting as well as I could."

To which one might add: His earliest submissions date from the summer of 1934, and included tales drawn from true-to-life Asian adventures, with characters roughly modeled on British/American intelligence operatives he had known in Shanghai. His early Westerns were similarly peppered with details drawn from personal experience. Although therein lay a first hard lesson from the often cruel world of the pulps. His first Westerns were soundly rejected as lacking the authenticity of a Max Brand yarn

Capt. L. Ron Hubbard in Ketchikan, Alaska, 1940, on his Alaskan Radio Experimental Expedition, the first of three voyages conducted under the Explorers Club flag.

(a particularly frustrating comment given L. Ron Hubbard's Westerns came straight from his Montana homeland, while Max Brand was a mediocre New York poet named Frederick Schiller Faust, who turned out implausible six-shooter tales from the terrace of an Italian villa).

Nevertheless, and needless to say, L. Ron Hubbard persevered and soon earned a reputation as among the most publishable names in pulp fiction, with a ninety percent placement rate of first-draft manuscripts. He was also among the most prolific, averaging between seventy and a hundred thousand words a month. Hence the rumors that L. Ron Hubbard had redesigned a typewriter for faster keyboard action and pounded out manuscripts on a continuous roll of butcher paper to save the precious seconds it took to insert a single sheet of paper into manual typewriters of the day.

That all L. Ron Hubbard stories did not run beneath said byline is yet another aspect of pulp fiction lore. That is, as publishers periodically rejected manuscripts from top-drawer authors if only to avoid paying top dollar, L. Ron Hubbard and company just as frequently replied with submissions under various pseudonyms. In Ron's case, the

---

A MAN OF MANY NAMES

Between 1934 and 1950, L. Ron Hubbard authored more than fifteen million words of fiction in more than two hundred classic publications. To supply his fans and editors with stories across an array of genres and pulp titles, he adopted fifteen pseudonyms in addition to his already renowned L. Ron Hubbard byline.

Winchester Remington Colt
Lt. Jonathan Daly
Capt. Charles Gordon
Capt. L. Ron Hubbard
Bernard Hubbel
Michael Keith
Rene Lafayette
Legionnaire 148
Legionnaire 14830
Ken Martin
Scott Morgan
Lt. Scott Morgan
Kurt von Rachen
Barry Randolph
Capt. Humbert Reynolds

---

list included: Rene Lafayette, Captain Charles Gordon, Lt. Scott Morgan and the notorious Kurt von Rachen—supposedly on the lam for a murder rap, while hammering out two-fisted prose in Argentina. The point: While L. Ron Hubbard as Ken Martin spun stories of Southeast Asian intrigue, LRH as Barry Randolph authored tales of romance on the Western range—which, stretching between a dozen genres is how he came to stand among the two hundred elite authors providing close to a million tales through the glory days of American Pulp Fiction.

L. Ron Hubbard, circa 1930, at the outset of a literary career that would finally span half a century.

In evidence of exactly that, by 1936 L. Ron Hubbard was literally leading pulp fiction's elite as president of New York's American Fiction Guild. Members included a veritable pulp hall of fame: Lester "Doc Savage" Dent, Walter "The Shadow" Gibson, and the legendary Dashiell Hammett—to cite but a few.

Also in evidence of just where L. Ron Hubbard stood within his first two years on the American pulp circuit: By the spring of 1937, he was ensconced in Hollywood, adopting a Caribbean thriller for Columbia Pictures, remembered today as *The Secret of Treasure Island*. Comprising fifteen thirty-minute episodes, the L. Ron Hubbard screenplay led to the most profitable matinée serial in Hollywood history. In accord with Hollywood culture, he was thereafter continually called upon

The 1937 Secret of Treasure Island, *a fifteen-episode serial adapted for the screen by L. Ron Hubbard from his novel,* Murder at Pirate Castle.

to rewrite/doctor scripts—most famously for long-time friend and fellow adventurer Clark Gable.

In the interim—and herein lies another distinctive chapter of the L. Ron Hubbard story—he continually worked to open Pulp Kingdom gates to up-and-coming authors. Or, for that matter, anyone who wished to write. It was a fairly unconventional stance, as markets were already thin and competition razor sharp. But the fact remains, it was an L. Ron Hubbard hallmark that he vehemently lobbied on behalf of young authors—regularly supplying instructional articles to trade journals, guest-lecturing to short story classes at George Washington University and Harvard, and even founding his own creative writing competition. It was established in 1940, dubbed the Golden Pen, and guaranteed winners both New York representation and publication in *Argosy*.

But it was John W. Campbell Jr.'s *Astounding Science Fiction* that finally proved the most memorable LRH vehicle. While every fan of L. Ron Hubbard's galactic epics undoubtedly knows the story, it nonetheless bears repeating: By late 1938, the pulp publishing magnate of Street & Smith was determined to revamp *Astounding Science Fiction* for broader readership. In particular, senior editorial director F. Orlin Tremaine called for stories with a stronger *human element*. When acting editor John W. Campbell balked, preferring his spaceship-driven tales, Tremaine enlisted Hubbard. Hubbard, in turn, replied with the genre's first truly *character-driven* works, wherein heroes are pitted not against bug-eyed monsters but the mystery and majesty of deep space itself—and thus was launched the Golden Age of Science Fiction.

The names alone are enough to quicken the pulse of any science fiction aficionado, including LRH friend and protégé, Robert Heinlein, Isaac Asimov, A. E. van Vogt and Ray Bradbury. Moreover, when coupled with LRH stories of fantasy, we further come to what's rightly been described as the foundation of every modern tale of horror: L. Ron Hubbard's immortal *Fear.* It was rightly proclaimed by Stephen King as one of the very few works to genuinely warrant that overworked term "classic"—as in: *"This is a classic tale of creeping, surreal menace and horror. . . . This is one of the really, really good ones."*

L. Ron Hubbard, 1948, among fellow science fiction luminaries at the World Science Fiction Convention in Toronto.

To accommodate the greater body of L. Ron Hubbard fantasies, Street & Smith inaugurated *Unknown*—a classic pulp if there ever was one, and wherein readers were soon thrilling to the likes of *Typewriter in the Sky* and *Slaves of Sleep* of which Frederik Pohl would declare: *"There are bits and pieces from Ron's work that became part of the language in ways that very few other writers managed."*

And, indeed, at J. W. Campbell Jr.'s insistence, Ron was regularly drawing on themes from the Arabian Nights and so introducing readers to a world of genies, jinn, Aladdin and Sinbad—all of which, of course, continue to float through cultural mythology to this day.

At least as influential in terms of post-apocalypse stories was L. Ron Hubbard's 1940 *Final Blackout*. Generally acclaimed as the finest anti-war novel of the decade and among the ten best works of the genre ever authored—here, too, was a tale that would live on in ways few other writers imagined.

Portland, Oregon, 1943; L. Ron Hubbard, captain of the US Navy subchaser PC 815.

Hence, the later Robert Heinlein verdict: "Final Blackout *is as perfect a piece of science fiction as has ever been written.*"

Like many another who both lived and wrote American pulp adventure, the war proved a tragic end to Ron's sojourn in the pulps. He served with distinction in four theaters and was highly decorated for commanding corvettes in the North Pacific. He was also grievously wounded in combat, lost many a close friend and colleague and thus resolved to say farewell to pulp fiction and devote himself to what it had supported these many years—namely, his serious research.

But in no way was the LRH literary saga at an end, for as he wrote some thirty years later, in 1980:

"Recently there came a period when I had little to do. This was novel in a life so crammed with busy years, and I decided to amuse myself by writing a novel that was pure *science fiction."*

That work was *Battlefield Earth: A Saga of the Year 3000.* It was an immediate *New York Times* bestseller and, in fact, the first international science fiction blockbuster in decades. It was not, however, L. Ron Hubbard's magnum opus, as that distinction is generally reserved for his next and final work: The 1.2 million word *Mission Earth.*

> **Final Blackout**
> *is as perfect a piece of science fiction as has ever been written.*
>
> —Robert Heinlein

How he managed those 1.2 million words in just over twelve months is yet another piece of the L. Ron Hubbard legend. But the fact remains, he did indeed author a ten-volume *dekalogy* that lives in publishing history for the fact that each and every volume of the series was also a *New York Times* bestseller.

Moreover, as subsequent generations discovered L. Ron Hubbard through republished works and novelizations of his screenplays, the mere fact of his name on a cover signaled an international bestseller. . . . Until, to date, sales of his works exceed hundreds of millions, and he otherwise remains among the most enduring and widely read authors in literary history. Although as a final word on the tales of L. Ron Hubbard, perhaps it's enough to simply reiterate what editors told readers in the glory days of American Pulp Fiction:

He writes the way he does, brothers, because he's been there, seen it and done it!

THE STORIES FROM THE GOLDEN AGE

Your ticket to adventure starts here with the Stories from the Golden Age collection by master storyteller L. Ron Hubbard. These gripping tales are set in a kaleidoscope of exotic locales and brim with fascinating characters, including some of the most vile villains, dangerous dames and brazen heroes you'll ever get to meet.

The entire collection of over one hundred and fifty stories is being released in a series of eighty books and audiobooks. For an up-to-date listing of available titles, go to www.goldenagestories.com.

AIR ADVENTURE

Arctic Wings	*Man-Killers of the Air*
The Battling Pilot	*On Blazing Wings*
Boomerang Bomber	*Red Death Over China*
The Crate Killer	*Sabotage in the Sky*
The Dive Bomber	*Sky Birds Dare!*
Forbidden Gold	*The Sky-Crasher*
Hurtling Wings	*Trouble on His Wings*
The Lieutenant Takes the Sky	*Wings Over Ethiopia*

FAR-FLUNG ADVENTURE

SEA ADVENTURE

118

TALES FROM THE ORIENT

MYSTERY

FANTASY

Borrowed Glory   *If I Were You*
The Crossroads   *The Last Drop*
Danger in the Dark   *The Room*
The Devil's Rescue   *The Tramp*
He Didn't Like Cats

SCIENCE FICTION

The Automagic Horse   *A Matter of Matter*
Battle of Wizards   *The Obsolete Weapon*
Battling Bolto   *One Was Stubborn*
The Beast   *The Planet Makers*
Beyond All Weapons   *The Professor Was a Thief*
A Can of Vacuum   *The Slaver*
The Conroy Diary   *Space Can*
The Dangerous Dimension   *Strain*
Final Enemy   *Tough Old Man*
The Great Secret   *240,000 Miles Straight Up*
Greed   *When Shadows Fall*
The Invaders

WESTERN

Encounter the Spectacular in Unusual Adventures!

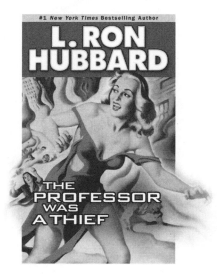

Primed for promotion to the *World-Journal* city editor (and an overdue raise), grizzled senior reporter Pop is stunned when it's announced that young Leonard Caulborn, the publisher's ambitious son-in-law, will get the post. Worse, the lad wants him out. In protest, Pop demands to be given a beat again and gets his wish . . . only now he's got just two days to find the "real" story about a dead-end assignment—a month-old physics lecture—or be fired.

When Pop starts searching for the story's source, an odd physics professor named Pertwee, he lands in the middle of the story of the century after the Empire State Building, Grant's Tomb and Grand Central Station all disappear. Apparently, Pertwee's the mastermind behind it all. But Pop soon discovers that, instead of inventing a new way to blow things up, the professor may be doing quite the opposite.